The God of Lies

Raven sipped the wine; it was soft and dry; refreshing.

The man sat down on the edge of the bed, smiling at her.

Raven looked at him, admiring his figure, enticed by his voice and eyes.

She looked again at the eyes. And saw that they had no pupils: were, merely, pools of blue without center or focus other than the hypnotic stare emanating like the sun's gaze from the blank centers.

"You lie!"

Abruptly, as she said it, the wine turned to bitter acid in her mouth.

She spat it out, gagging on the sour taste . . .

"Of course I lie. I am the god of lies. I can turn your life into a lie. I can lay with you if I choose, but you are yet too petty a little human. You must learn my ways before I favor you."

There was a darkness deeper than before. Not night, not shuttered windows, nor closing doors, but absence of life. Raven whimpered in fear, her body chilled by the anger of the creature.

"And you will learn!" The voice echoed like thunder about the invisible confines of the blank room.

Ace Fantasy books by Richard Kirk

A TIME OF DYING

RICHARD KIRK

ACE BOOKS, NEW YORK

This Ace book contains the complete
text of the original edition.
It has been completely reset in a typeface
designed for easy reading and was printed
from new film.

RAVEN 5: A TIME OF DYING

An Ace Book/published by arrangement with
the author

PRINTING HISTORY
Corgi edition published 1979
Ace edition/January 1988

ISBN: 0-441-70575-8

Ace Books are published by The Berkley Publishing Group,
200 Madison Avenue, New York, New York 10016.
The name "ACE" and the "A" logo
are trademarks belonging to Charter Communications, Inc.
PRINTED IN THE UNITED STATES OF AMERICA

10 9 8 7 6 5 4 3 2 1

For she whose name must not be spoken

QUWHON

THE
ICE WASTES

Frost Water

North Water

THE
LOST LANDS

River Ish

THE
RIFT

ISHKAR

DARK ISLANDS

Black
Lake

Black Water

SIY

River Shima

Lake Xand

Haral

XANDRONE
• Yin

Horn River

Uthaa

Spygan

WORLD'S
END
MOUNTAIN

River Utho

VALLEY OF
UTHAAN

Prologue

Once, farther back in time than any could remember, in a past grown misty with forgotten memories, the place had been a palace. Even now, despite the ravages of age and elements, of the land itself, the outlines might be discerned by those with the eyes to see and the knowledge of that vision's objective. The walls were long gone in ruin, the great stone blocks tumbled down like the marble pillars and the many-hued tiles that had decorated the roofs. The timbers and the metals, the jewels that had sparkled from the towering buttresses, the statuary and the frescoes, all were gone. Later builders had pillaged the ruins for materials with which to fabricate simpler dwelling places; not palaces, for the time of palaces was past.

Sun and wind and rain had worked their eroding spell. Roots from the great trees, and the smaller, faster tendons of vines and creepers had joined the combat. In its own death throes the palace had seeded its demise, the massive blocks falling to choke the wells and alter the course of the streams and springs that had fed the place its water, causing that same life-giving fluid to burst forth from the ground in new directions, gnawing like so many non-corporate rodents at the foundations.

Now grass flourished where once there had been pavements of malachite and amethyst. Vines strangled columns of unfeeling marble, creepers wound languid arms about chunks of dead stone. Crepulescent weeds clogged the wells, covering the stagnant water with a miasic layer of spongy, iridescent filth so thick that rats and toads ran or hopped carelessly over the bluish-green mats.

Yet still, for those with the eyes to see, the outlines of

1

the palace were visible. A wall here, the grassy mound of a fallen tower there; a patch of broken paving where yellow and red flowers divided the flagstones; a darker patch amongst the greenery, where a fireplace had heated a great hall; a gulley that had once been a cistern or a cellar.

Those with eyes to see . . .

Eyes that blink dimly from a withered, aged skull . . .

Or the eyes that look inwards to re-create from the cobwebs of the past a present unreality that still makes visible that which no longer exists.

"It was a kinder place, once. A place of laughter and love. Not this stinking cess-pit."

The old man shrugged his shoulders, still broad despite the weight of innumerable years, and dabbled a hand in a rivulet of clear water, smiling an old, timeless smile.

The men with him grinned at one another, anticipating a new story, for the oldster they had found wandering carelessly through the forest had a store of such musings as filled the sweltering hours of noonday or the slow, still twilights with fantasy.

Who he was, they knew not. Nor cared overmuch. They were merchants, intent only on trading what few goods they had with the few scattered villages cut from this horrible jungle. Yet even merchants, hard-headed traders with swift swords and tightly-locked purse strings, can enjoy a story. And if the old man was able to transmute his stories into gold, then he would have been worth the robbing for the chests of wealth he must have toted with him.

Yet few there were who might have dared such a venture, for old as he was, there was that about him that forbade such mercenary inclinations. His face was seamed across with wrinkles as deep and as old as the cracks in the stones on which they sat, his skin pale and taut on a visage still handsome. A mane of silver hair spread down from a high forehead over shoulders once well-used to swordwork, and his eyes remained bright as the sky they could barely see: pale blue, azure, and swift in their gaze as the look of a stooping hawk. His right hand was a stump wrapped in dirty cloth, the confines of the material indicating where fingers had been hacked from his palm. But his left, the tendons standing corded out of the aged skin, was never far from the hilt of the sword he carried.

That sword alone would pay a year's journeying, for there were none such made now. Nor any in as long as the merchants could remember, though occasionally—if a man was very lucky—a similar blade might be uncovered in some burial mound or desecrated tomb. If any tombs were left undesecrated.

It was a sword long as a man's arm, the blade an undimmed silver, despite its obvious age. The hilt of it was wrapped all around with golden wire, the pommel set with a huge, green-glowing gemstone. The guard—straight bar with cup—was of a metal unknown to the merchants, silver as the blade itself, and topped with little points of yellow metal. The thing was held in a plain leather scabbard, mildew fusting the sheath with greenish fur, yet the blade itself gave no sign of ageing. Both edges were razor-sharp, and though the dark, tell-tale stains of blood showed in the central groove, there was no corrosion. It was as if the sword belonged to a different time; had been snatched loose to exist for ever in a kind of limbo, unageing; ageless.

The old man touched his damp palm to the hilt and smiled as the contact flooded remembrance through his mind.

"The weeds have taken over the earth, and from the mud the poisons are come loose." His voice was husky; dry like dust, yet moist with memory. *"I can remember when this place where we live was cleaner. When giant deeds were done, and a man stood upright on his own two feet and trusted his swordarm to call the tune of the world's dancing. We left the crawling of merchants to those best fitted to the purpose, then. And those who found their hands matched a blade more suitably than a contract took up the blade and used it.*

"Raven was such a one. Such a woman as you poor traders shall never know. A woman of gold and death. The woman of dreams and desire. A woman who belongs to the past and the future."

He chuckled, the sound dry and dusty in the solemn heat of noonday.

"She might bed you or kill you. In equal measure. She knew love in equal measure with death, could thrust and slay; or turn her body to catch the eye as surely as a trap will take a deer or a fish. She turned worlds, that one. And worlds turned upon her."

"Were her dugs as large as that Sowestrian whore we favoured yesternight?" The youngest of the merchants touched his crotch in obscene manner. "Did she perform so well with three men on her?"

"Your tongue is glib enough to slime your lips like the passage of a slug. Which is your mind," said the old man. *"I do not speak of whores, but of a woman, the like of which the world we know had never seen. Nor will again."*

He paused, dipping the stump of his hand into the turgid water. The young merchant came to his feet, a blade darting clear of the scabbard slung across his shoulders.

He was still rising as the long silver blade darted from the rotting scabbard and pricked its point through the cloth of his robe, so that a tiny circle of red gusted out between his navel and his crotch.

The old man shifted his arm, tucking the bright silver blade a fraction deeper into the flesh. The young man drew back his lips in horrid semblance of a smile, and paced back from the needle point of the sword.

"We outnumber you, old man." His voice was uncertain as he saw that his companions made no move to join him. "Can you slay us all?"

"It is not impossible." The old voice was firmer now, definite in its menace. *"But before you choose your fate listen to what I say. Then decide if death holds so much glamour that you should embrace her darkness so eagerly."*

The young merchant drew farther back, uncertain, glancing round for support. None came, and he sheathed his sword with an angry grunt.

"Sit down," murmured the old man, lowering the gem-hilted blade. *"Sit down and listen to things you cannot understand. I shall tell how easily death may visit you. And how death may be defeated. Perhaps you will learn something from the telling. I doubt it, because the world is young now. It was older then, the puppies listened to wisdom."*

A merchant chuckled, filling a leather cup with sour wine, passing it to the ancient yarn-spinner. The other two nodded approval, settling back on mildewed saddles to hear the tale. The young man shrugged, fiddling with his sword, but even his attention was caught, his anger near-forgot. The old man let the great sword rest on the grass, his eyes assuming a hazed, long-distant look.

"I shall tell you," he said slowly, *"of how I met death. And of how death died."*

One

"On the back of the wind. On the back of Xand. We
come with horns and hooves and steel. We bring death."
Xand Riders' Song.

It was the time of the Summer Gathering.

From all the far-flung horn-holds of Xandrone the riders
and the herders came in to Srygar and Xin and Haral. They
came with herds for trading, stallions and female Xands
for breeding stock; plump calves for eating or buying; with
fighting Xands, the horns tipped with needle-pointed metal,
or the natural sharpness of trained ivory. With Xands
trained to haul a wagon, their resistance gone with their
testicles.

The three cities of the Horn River filled up with a
mewling, bellowing, cacophonous spill of hairy men, lithe-
limbed women and urgent, often-angry beasts.

Chaos reigned.

Over Haral, chiefest of the cities, there hung a thick,
almost tangible mist. It was compounded of Xand sweat
and that of the riders; of sweet Saran wine and the more
bitter pungency of Xandronian gryllar, the rough, mind-
bursting liquor favoured by the riders. There was a hint of
moist furs and sweat-dampened leather; of steel from
Tirwand and Quwhon; and one of the soft silks of Sara and
Lyand and Vartha'an.

The odours of cooking lifted high enough—and thick
enough—to match those of the liquors. Steaks of Xand and
Yr; of pungent glara, and succulent s'ymstal. Of the costly
ba'ndath, that roasted on massive spits with the names of
the fishermen from Haral and the Dark Islands who had
died bringing the sea-beasts to land painted alongside the
prices; which were very high, for the flesh of the ba'ndath
settled the debts of the wailing mothers and wives and
children.

There was also sound. And perhaps that overtopped even the smells and the movement.

It was the sound of thousands. Of feet and hooves and voices and bellowing. Of fylar harps and Xandronian flutes. Of muttered conversations and shouted arguments. Of Quwhon metal on Tirwanian steel. Of blood, and the soft, sticky sounds of dying. The sound of voices chanting a bet on a contestant in a personal combat; or the greater roar of a crowd that watched two Xands gore blood from one another.

But most of all, it was the sound and the smell and the movement of the cattle-things, for Xandrone was given over to the raising of the horned beasts, and they were meat and armour and weapons and gods.

Great, they were. Higher than a horse, standing two heads' length taller than the biggest stallion that even the Altanate could boast. Heavy of shoulder and chest, the ribs so wide that even the tallest of men must hike his heels to the upward stirrups set against the top joint of the limbs, and rest his spine against the high, couch-like saddle that protected him at front and back and sides. Hairy, like some monkey from the jungles of the Ishkar Rift, but graced with curving horns the full spread of a man's body, from skull to toes, or longer. Their heads were flat and bovine, only the red eyes indicating the fury that might be unleashed at a moment's anger, or the master's bidding, the mouths toothed with flat, grass-cropping ivory that could crunch a bone as easily as they might crop the verdancy of the massive, wide-spreading plains that spread all the way from the Worldheart Ocean to the World's End Mountains, from the boundaries of the Utha River to the Shima.

Their hooves were three-toed, the end points sharp enough to gut and disembowel. And their tails were heavy with fur, laced with muscle powerful enough to strike a man unconscious at a single blow.

Slower than a horse at full gallop, the Xands could run for longer by three times than the fastest, or most enduring horse. They needed only grass and water to exist. And their hides—so prized as armour—were impervious as steel to the assault of weapons.

Thus it was that Karhsaam and the Southern Cities of Lyand, Sara, and Vartha'an all had boats in the harbour of Haral.

Not only cattle boats, but also grain boats. For the Xands could exist only on the grasses of Xandrone, so that any warlord seeking to employ the massive weight and power of the huge beasts must also purchase the stocks set up throughout the summer by the Xandronian grain traders. And then protect his purchases from the depredations of Kragg pirates, or greedy City States with war boats.

So the town of Haral, at the mouth of the Horn River, was filled up with sea captains and warriors. With marine mercenaries in the employ of the Altan, and more from the Southern Cities; with traders from Lym and Irkar, Ghorm and Zantar; even from Sen and Tul and Ish in wild, lost Ishkar.

Black women from Sly, their cheeks tattooed with designs in red and blue and yellow, danced with armour-clad soldiers from Balim and Gath and Karhsaam, dark breasts, naked of adornment other than the tattoo punctures, pressed hard to plates of steel or Xand hide. Soft, blonde women, all silks and slitted eyes, wove seductive paces about hairy Xand riders, who laughed and dragged the women down, screaming, into the hay of the stalls.

Even the sea-reivers of Kragg were there, sporting furs and chainmail, their hands never far from axe or sword, but still laughing, still enjoying. Like the men of Ishkar and the few come in from Sly, they drank deep and long. Took their pleasure where they found it, and as much again if anyone complained.

It was the time of the Summer Gathering. Not a time for civilised niceties, nor the usual rules of a city.

And in a dark corner of Haral, close against the walls where the shadows were longest at evening, and soonest come, a thing stirred.

The thing had been waiting. For how long, it could not know: time was meaningless to such as this, of no importance to its conception of reality. It knew only purpose.

It was a tall, dark, shapeless thing that lurched up from the mud and sewer-stink of a ditch and dragged itself slowly up the steep bank. Leeches fell from its body—if body was what it had—and withered, dying on the poison-ous nourishment sucked from its flesh. Near tall as a Xand, it was, with glowing eyes and a hint of phosphores-cence about its feet and hands, as though gleaming claws hung there, pulsing.

It rested for a moment on the bank, drinking in the stink of rotting fish and ageing Xand hides as a man might savour the scent of fresh flowers or new-cut grass. Then it climbed to its feet and paced slowly towards the nearest house.

The door burst open when the thing swung one arm against the wood. The timber scorched and sprang in-wards, lock exploding as hinges melted and fell away. There were dark, red-rimmed lines across the wood.

The woman inside screamed and put an arm about her child.

The boy was little more than four years old. Strong for his age, and swifter than most. His name was Tal van Darth, and already he had ridden a baby Xand with his father's help. Gar'Tal van Darth was then pitting his own trained Xand against a mottled beast from the highlands west of Klingse, though as the winning stroke cut through the animal's neck and assured him of five hundred dalrs, he experienced a curious sensation of unease, and took it to mind that he should hurry home.

When he arrived he was partly drunk on gryllar.

When he saw his home he sobered instantly with the emptying of his stomach.

The door of the little house was gone. It appeared to have been shattered by a lightning bolt, split into several parts and hurled inwards. The table too, was destroyed, as was the window, the glass and frame all mangled together in fragments.

Down one wall there dripped a thick, ugly stream of stinking red. The same putrescence draped the window frame and the floor and the bed. Worst of all was the odour of corpses, like a charnel house opened up and exposed to the sun.

Gar'Tal van Darth stumbled over something lying on the floor. He fell down, cursing, reaching for his knife. Then he saw what it was he had fallen over, and opened his mouth afresh to vomit his fear and disgust over the stained planks.

His wife's head rested close by his face. Part of her body was still upon the bed, though most of it was littered about the room. His son's corpse was in similar disarray: a limb caught on the windowledge, another tossed against a light hung from the rearward wall, the head set between the mother's torn legs. There was nothing of either of them that could be properly called human, only pieces, like joints of meat in a butcher's shop.

Gar'Tal van Darth swung his head back and screamed. He went on screaming until his neighbours came in and found him, and took him away with three strong men holding him down against his madness.

And the thing moved on through the Night of the Summer Gathering.

Twelve there were who died in Haral that night, so that in after times the city came to call it the Night of the Blood. Though for a long time after, there was none could put a face on the ravening beast that stalked the festive streets and transmuted joyous laughter to bloody tears. And for longer still, none who would dare track the thing and risk his life in slaying it.

Or them, for it was difficult to tell how many there might be: whether one, or several.

The family of Danan ta Eele was next to fall. Father, mother and two children slaughtered as they sat down to their evening meal.

Then Van ta Kirith, who was drunk on Saran wine and stumbling home with a slave girl called Iri in his arms. Iri died too.

After them a coachman known only as Fass, who died with the Xand he used to pull his coach, and all three of his passengers. Two men—Vur van Twem and Nayal ta Ylim—along with the whore they shared, a girl known as Lys the Golden.

Gold became red that night, and Lys lost all her trade for ever as she was rent apart and spread over the street, like offal tossed out for the dogs.

There was no pattern to the killing. No differentiation

between rich and poor, high-born or commoner. It was as though madness stalked the streets of the festival city and sought to kill joy. As though a demon walked loose from the bowels of the lowest hell. And soon the word spread, and folk locked their doors, or moved abroad in groups, with hands on swords and throwing stars, ready for attack. The council of the city increased the patrols, whose more usual duty was to stem the bloodier of the fights and control those men become overly violent in their cups. But few fights broke out, and few men cared to risk drunkenness when such laxity might mean bloody death rather than a brief spell in the dungeons of Haral.

Dawn brought a measure of peace, though the festivities had lost that buoyant carelessness that marked the Summer Gathering as a time of joyful madness.

During the day the trading went on, as trading will no matter what grim fate threatens; the Xand combats continued, as did the races; gamblers still wagered on beasts or men or dice; and the stalls went on selling their sweetmeats and fish and liquor. But it was not the same, and as twilight descended over the sprawling city there was a marked increase in the number of torches lit that made more noticeable the lessening of the crowds thronging the streets.

And five more people died.

The festival continued through Second Day and Torch Day, through the crowning of the Xand King and the enthronement of Xand Queen. The Day of Sacrifice passed and Farewell Day came, marking the termination of the Gathering.

By that time full thirty people had bade farewell to life itself.

It was the saddest Gathering any could remember, even the oldest, silver-bearded inhabitants of the city. The merchants complained of loss of revenue. The people complained of fear. Dyn ta Kell, who was that year's Guardian, complained that he lacked the men to patrol every alleyway and secluded plaza. And the council complained that the Guardian had failed in his duty, that tithe was lost along with face. The priests of the Horn Temple wailed and doubled their sacrificing; it was even mooted that a return to the old ways should be considered, and a virgin found to placate whatever demon vented its wrath on Haral.

The Gathering ended, and with it, the killings. The city drew in its breath, waiting.

A year passed.

The grass grew thick and lush, affording a better harvest than had been known since the days of Old Catar. The herds multiplied in unvisioned quantities, and all the beasts were of prime quality. The herald boats of Xandrone went out from Haral harbour, spreading word along the coastal towns of Worldheart. Riders took it inland, and river barges, so that it passed northwards to distant Ish and east to Lym and Balim, to Heldan and Karhsaam.

And—as is ever the case—memory dimmed fear in contrast to profit: merchants began to gather afresh, though many brought with them bodyguards, or whole packs of mercenaries. The representatives of the Altan attended with two full squads of hired swords from Ishkar and Lorn; and it was even rumoured that a troop of Beastmen from the Rift was held in reserve at the palace rented by the Altan's Jedda. Once again, the flat-bottomed merchantmen of the Southern Cities rubbed caulked planks with the lean wolfboats of Kragg, the high-prowed galleys of Karhsoam, and the wide-hulled scows of Sen and Tul and Ish. Horsemen rode in from Uthak, from Yr and Tirwand, from the faraway Lost Lands that bordered cold Quwhon on her western flank.

In the time it takes for a world to turn from summer to summer, aided by the drowsy heat and the promise of profit and amusement, roseate memory set a comforting, dimming overlay on fear.

Dyn ta Kell, who was still the City Guardian, persuaded the council to set forth larger funding for his men. The patrols were quadrupled, and each man was voted a band of throwing stars together with a good sword, a shield, and a light javelin.

The Horn priests doubled their sacrifices, sending up prayers to every Xandronian deity they could recall from the Tomes of the Horn, so that for a month before the

Gathering Haral was layered with pungent smoke and the odour of blood.

The riders began to gather, for of all the cities of the river, Haral was the greatest, the place where a breeder would find the best price for his stock; a grain merchant the best offer for his stored grass; a trainer, the most lucrative employ; or a fighter, the richest rewards. Similarly, the stallmen knew that few questions were asked about the price of a ba'ndath slice, or a piece of grilled s'ymstal; for a mug of gryllar or a flask of imported Saran wine. The out-city traders shared that avaricious optimism, arriving early enough to rent their shops, or market positions in anticipation of unloading their wares, so that Haral became filled again with colour and life.

The plazas filled with gaily coloured stalls that sold soft rich silks or hard, cool steel. Tempting foods; narcotic weeds that offered a spell of restful oblivion; or pungent liquors that offered instant oblivion and a sore head. There were doctors claiming knowledge of Kharwan's secrets, and priests from Quell vying with those who worshipped the All-Mother or the Tower of the dark gods of the Southern Wastes.

Once again, Haral came alive.

The man and the woman who had stepped down the gangplank of a scow from Tul exchanged a cynical smile as they strolled by the multiplicity of images decorating the plaza of the gods.

They appeared, to the casual eye, no more than any other pair of sightseers come to enjoy the abandonment of the Summer Gathering. Long, soft cloaks of heavy-spun silk covered them from throat to ankle, the man's dark as deepest midnight, the woman's a green susurration like the waves of the sea on the shores of the Dark Islands. Each one carried a satchel of soft Yr leather slung across the shoulder: the left shoulder. And they chinked faintly as they walked, as though the satchels, or hidden pouches, held coins of some weight.

The woman was near tall as the man. A magnificent creature, whose feminine contours defied even the cloak's hiding. Her face, smiling, was lipped wide and full be-

neath a firm, straight nose. Her eyes were blue, like a
misty sea, rather than a summer sky: blue and green and
grey mingled together beneath dark lashes that curved in
sultry density above the wide orbs of her vision. Her hair
was thick and long and golden, like the radiance of the sun
as it begins to pale on a summer twilight. A circle of
platinum bound it back from her face, so that it fell over
her shoulders and curled about the swell of her breasts
beneath the cloak, falling down to her waist, beneath
which twin globes of enticement danced rhythmically as
she matched her companion's stride.

Had the ogle-eyed watchers been able to concentrate
their stares to penetrate the cloak, they would have seen
long, firm legs, booted to the upper part of smooth, sun-
kissed thighs with Yr leather. A short kirtle, slit at either
side for freedom of movement, and belted to a narrow
waist with a wide belt into which was mounted a string of
throwing stars. They might have seen the silken blouse,
the colour of dark cream, that was tugged tight by the
swell of her breasts, fastened loose about her neck so that
it hung down to expose the tempting shadows between
those mounds. And the slender dagger of dark Quwhonian
steel fastened below the belt of stars.

The man was a head taller, his visage lean as though
poised between hunger and satisfaction. His hair, unbound,
fell down in thick, black folds about his face and shoulders. His eyes were blue; not the misty shade of the
woman's, but a pure, translucent azure that might almost
become silver in the sun. His mouth was wide and firm,
with a hardness about it that was offset only by the curva-
ture of his smile. He was slender, long of leg and arm, yet
muscled in hard cords that danced on the surface of his
pale skin in easy rhythm. Beneath his cloak he wore a
tunic of black, decorated with protective linkages of silver
chain, fastened at the throat with a silver brooch, and
reaching below his waist. His legs were clad in leather
breeches of black Yr hide, worked soft and tucked into
knee-high boots of the same material. About his narrow
waist was a simple belt with a sheathed dagger and a silver
buckle scribed with runes.

Although they were obviously together and obviously

enjoying a shared affection—they walked a pace apart, each one leaving sufficient space that a blade might be drawn from beneath the cloaks, or the satchels opened swiftly.

One priest—more anxious to proselytise than his fellows, or perhaps less cautious—darted out from his stall, shaking a rattle in their faces and mumbling incantations. He danced before them, moving back as they strode on, spreading his arms to block their passing as he peered up, lips still moving.

"It appears we are required to halt and listen to this ranting." The man smiled, glancing at the woman. "Shall we spend a moment, Raven? Or find some place to stay?"

Amused, the woman called Raven shrugged, the movement stirring her cloak, so the priest halted his prattling as he caught sight of her body.

"Listen awhile, Spellbinder. Surely we have time enough for finding beds."

"Bed," corrected the dark man. "And food, for my belly rumbles with the thought of decent victuals. However . . ." He looked down at the capering priest. "Speak on."

"I follow the Lord Vedast." The priest was little more than thirty summers of age, yet stooped over and balding beneath his circlet of plaited leather. "The only Lord able to protect you from the Black One."

Spellbinder frowned, ignoring the chuckle of his companion.

"Which Black One?" he asked. "I have heard of too many black ones to differentiate overmuch."

"Him of the darkness! The One who comes in the night to rend and destroy. The soul stealer. The one that turned last First Night to the Night of the Blood. Lord Vedast may offer you his protection."

Spellbinder shrugged. "I know not this Lord Vedast or this Black One. We are strangers to Haral, unfamiliar with your customs."

The priest twirled round in a shuffling circle, drumming his rattle with renewed vigour.

"Best seek protection, then, outlanders. Seek it now, lest the nightcomer takes you. For only seven dalrs I will weave a spell about you that will hold you clean-free of the Black One. For seven more, I can make you disciples of the Lord Vedast.''

Raven laughed out loud. ''This god of yours is not so anxious, then, to find disciples that he gives his favours freely? He must be bought? Perhaps this Black One may be purchased with the same coin. Or honest steel.''

''Naked blasphemer!'' The priest crouched down, red-rimmed eyes glowering at the woman. ''Guard your tongue, outland whore, lest the Lord Vedast rip it from your painted mouth.''

Raven laughed again, but Spellbinder frowned.

''Guard your own tongue, priest, else some stronger magic be brought to work on you.''

''There is none stronger.'' The little man spat at Spellbinder's boots. ''The Lord Vedast is all. Spend your seven dalrs, or be forever cursed.''

''With avarice?'' Spellbinder asked quietly, shrugging his cloak from his shoulders so that his arms and hands were exposed. ''Like you?''

He muttered beneath his breath, using some incomprehensible language that baffled the ear with its complexity rather than its softness, and moved his hands in a swift, short pattern.

Abruptly the little priest ceased his prancing. He became as stone, unmoving, like a puppet suddenly frozen in middance. His face remained contorted with anger, one hand lifted up to wave the rattle above his immobile head, the other extended to point into space as Raven and Spellbinder strolled past him. The other priests murmured to themselves, making whatever sign belonged to their particular deity.

Raven and Spellbinder went on to the far side of the plaza, pausing as they reached the outer extremity at the dark man's request. He turned, twisting a hand before him and mouthing a secondary spell. The little priest sprang back to life, staring round in surprise and shouting high-pitched curses that had little to do with his Lord Vedast, though much with the gutter.

''Foolish little man,'' smiled Raven, twining an arm through Spellbinder's. ''Why waste spell-energy on him?''

The dark man licked his lips, shaking his head doubtfully.

"Foolish, yes," he agreed. "But still truthful. I sensed that about him when first he halted us. I held him in thrall long enough to seek a deeper kuowledge of what he said. I found truth there. There is a Black One."

Raven released his arm, her hand reaching instinctively beneath the cloak to touch the weapons couched there.

"Such as Tanash? Or Belthis? Surely not."

"I cannot say as yet," murmured Spellbinder. "All I sensed was a force and a knowledge. What form the thing takes, I cannot guess; only know it was here, and may come again."

"So will night and the following dawn." Raven attempted to lighten his mood. "And by then we should have food inside us and a bed on which to discuss such matters. Or others."

"Aye." Spellbinder smiled, shaking off his gloomy mood. "So it goes."

They set out along a wide avenue, following the directions given them by their boat captain to a tavern of respectable reputation, where rooms and food of equal quality might be found.

The Inn of the Horns was located in a quiet square a spear's cast from the central plaza of Haral, and to reach the hostelry they were required to traverse the busier part of the city, thus obtaining some impression of its size and demeanour.

It appeared a friendly, even homely place. The streets and avenues were wide to allow for the by-passing of the massive Xand-drawn carts that rutted the cobbles, lined with more narrow pavements from which trees grew. The houses and shops and drinking places flanking the pavements sported metal baskets of trailing flowers and vines, all red and green and purple. There were cages, too, hung on poles from the windows, containing tiny yellow and scarlet birds that filled the air with their song. The houses, like the drinking establishments, were entered through high gates of carved wood or fancifully wrought metal, like the streets, wide enough that a Xand might pass through. Smaller openings were sent into the main gates, for foot travellers, and these were guarded by armed men.

The city spread upwards from the docks built along the edge of the Horn river's estuary, the streets winding through buildings of wood or stone, few taller than two floors, though all richly carved with frescoes and alcoves in which busts or statues resided. The slope was steep enough that a man's legs got to aching before he reached the plateau on which the centre of Haral rested, and he might well pause to refresh himself along the way. From the plateau it was possible to see clear down to the waterfront, where the bright-pennanted ships and boats rested quiet on the incoming tide, though the central square itself was impressive enough that his eyes might be torn from that seaward gaze.

A quarter of a kli on every side, it was. Surrounded by the richest of all the buildings, and those dwarfed in both size and magnificence by the Temple of the Horns, the Chambers of the Council, and the Hall of the Guardian. A fountain, wrought of black Quwhon steel in the shape of a bellowing Xand, sprayed water in a stately jet over flower-banked terraces, and all around the plaza there were tables and chairs served by eager serving wenches and busy waiters. Four roadways converged on the plaza, one lifting up from the docks, a second from the inland regions, the others from north and south, so that they marked the points of the compass.

Raven and Spellbinder took the northern avenue, following it as instructed until they passed a quiet garden beside an open-fronted shop selling Xand-hide armour, saddles, and the other accoutrements of a rider. There they turned west down a narrow street that disgorged into the square containing the Inn of the Horns.

The hospice was marked by a Xand skull bearing a gigantic spread of yellowing ivory, half as wide again as a tall man with his arms lifted above his head. Beneath the craggy skull was a legend, carved into a plate of golden metal. It said: *This was Kanthus, mightiest of all Xands. Undefeated, he sired a thousand and died satisfied.*

Spellbinder translated the Xandronian script for Raven, who smiled and shrugged, mischievously.

"There are men would attempt the same prodigiousness, though perhaps lacking the spread of horn."

"Not I," grinned Spellbinder. "Though mayhap Gondar Lifebane would make the boast, or Quez M'yrstal."

"Gondar, perhaps," murmured Raven. "That sea-reiver would boast the same fathering; but not the Altan, not that pampered popinjay."

A shadow passed momentarily across her face, like a storm cloud scudding shadowy over golden wheat.

"Let's speak of more cheerful memories."

"Surely." Spellbinder nodded, hiking his satchel higher upon his shoulder, and smiling at the woman. "Let's speak of good food and better wine. A soft bed and a shared bath. And after those things are accomplishments, let's rest back and decide what amusement shall fill the night."

Raven laughed, her moment of depression lifted as swiftly as that same storm cloud might be blown from the same, honey-brown field of lush corn. She pushed her cloak back from her shoulders, reaching out to link her arm again with Spellbinder's. And together, side-by-side, they entered the courtyard of the Inn of the Horns.

They were met by a fat man, a Xandronian to judge by his short stature and hirsute appearance, dressed in faded leathers, with an apron belted around his girth.

"Welcome, strangers," he said. "Welcome from Taram van Bril. I can offer you the best food in all of Haral. And the finest wines. But if you seek a room, then it must be my eternal regret to disappoint you. The Inn has been filled nine passings since."

"Ga'grith Shanar," smiled Spellbinder, "told us a different tale when he brought us south on the *Maiden of Tul*. He said that the mere mention of his name would secure us a room. That and the price, of course."

As he said it, coins appeared in his hand, chinking together with the reassuring, solid sound of good Ishkarian gold.

The eyes of Taram van Bril grew wide as his smile, though that expression grew wider still.

"Ga'grith?" he spluttered. "That old pirate still plies his trade? You should have spoken his name earlier, stranger. Then I'd not have denied you hospitality. For friends of Ga'grith there is always room."

He turned about, executing a bow of surprising delicacy

for one so great of girth, and ushered them across the courtyard.

The gate through which they had entered the hostelry was timber built, heavy planks reinforced with bars of steel, locked with huge bolts. To either side were keep-huts, looking new-built against the weathered wood of the old gate. The yard was alternately cobbled and grassed, surrounded on three sides by the gate wall and those of the flanking buildings, on the fourth by the frontage of the inn itself. Beds of bright-hued flowers blazed colour from the feet of the walls, and a myriad large cages held flocks of the little yellow and red birds. A fountain—a miniature facsimile of the great font in the central plaza—occupied the middle space, its perimeter channelled to provide a drinking trough.

One half of the inn was given over to stables, and through the open doors Raven could see Xands penned up in stalls. The other half was full three storeys high, the roof crenellated with ornate woodwork and the wall punc-tured by shuttered windows, its woodwork covered with a spread of green and crimson vine that sprouted white flow-ers, imparting to the air a sweet, subtle perfume.

Inside, the place was cool and roomy, the doors opening on to a large hall set round with chairs and tapestries depicting the past glories of Xandrone. Taram van Bril led them past an alcove where a red-faced woman sat behind a scroll with a wall of keys at her back, and took them up the stairs that wound narrowly from the farther corner of the hall.

The stairs ran up to a landing that spread along the length of the rearward wall, a retaining panel rising from its floor to the ceiling, viewing slits cut into the panelling at regular intervals. The same confined balcony was dupli-cated on the second floor and the third, so that guests might look down, unseen, on the entry hall.

Their room was at the top of the building, set directly beneath the roof, with wide windows opening on to a balcony that was high enough to afford a view across the city. It was, for all Taram's excuses, one of the finest in the place. A broad, low-ceilinged room sported glassed doors opening on to the balcony. The floor was of rich-

polished timber, the reddish glow imparting a warmth of
feeling that was increased by the cool colours of the
white-dyed Xand hides spread over the wood. To one side
there was a low table, its simplicity denoting a master-
craftsman's work, as did the chairs and the low settle
arranged about the floor. A white-panelled door opened
into a bedroom, where a huge bed occupied the focal
space; above it, windows covered with filmy drapes, and
facing it, a wardrobe of gigantic size. Beyond that was a
bathroom. Tiled, in contrast to the wood of the other
rooms, and equipped with a deep, low-set tub that boasted
faucets at either end and sufficient space for a family to
bathe in. There were no windows in this room, but a
system of vents and fans that would remove the steam and
filter cooler air in at the turn of a carved wheel mounted in
the floor to one side of the tub.

It was a magnificent suite. And after the lonely tribula-
tions of the Lost Lands, and the long journey southwards,
it took away Raven's breath, reminding her of the luxuries
of the Altan's palace in far Karhsaam.

Taram van Bril left them there, promising the finest
meal they had ever eaten when the sun went down, one
that he would prepare himself in honour of their friendship
with Ga'grith Shanar.

Spellbinder followed the plump man to the door, then
whispered in his ear, curious. Taram's bland face grew
cloudy, and he shrugged off the murmuring as one who
rejects a bad memory, closing the door quickly so as to cut
off any further remembrance.

"What did you ask him?" Raven queried. "It seemed
to disturb his mind."

"It did." Spellbinder's voice was flat; ominous with
doubt. "I asked him about this Black One, that and the
Lord Vedast."

Raven was devoid of her cloak, and already slipping
free of her clothes. The tub was gurgling as it filled with
water, and the unguents and salts left in the bathroom
filled the rooms with a sensual odour.

"And what did he say?"

Her blouse fell to the floor, swiftly followed by her kirtle.

"What was it that sent him so fast from our company?"

Spellbinder went over to the windows, throwing them open to pace out on to the balcony where the view encompassed half of Haral in a single glimpse.

"He said that last Gathering thirty people died at the hand of some demon. That the Horn priests were unable to control it, as were the Guardian's patrols. He said that the followers of the Lord Vedast have appeared since that time, and claim controlling of the Black One."

He paused, staring across the city.

Then: "He did not wish to speak of it. He wanted to forget. But I sensed in his mind that he thinks it may come again."

Naked, Raven followed him through the tall windows, going behind him to join her arms about his waist, nestling her body to his, her cheek pressed to his shoulder.

"Does that concern us? Did we not agree that this Gathering was a time of forgetting?"

Spellbinder's head drooped, resting his chin upon his chest. He folded his arms to cup Raven's hands, which he kissed, gently.

"There is no forgetting. The world moves and shifts us with it. What we desire is nothing in comparison with the plan of the overworld."

Raven butted her chin against his back, grinding her body against him in mute protest.

"Once again you speak in the riddles of Kharwhan. *I* can forget if I wish. I am here, now, with you. That is all I want to remember. If the Priest-Kings of the Ghost Isle seek some turner of worlds, let them look elsewhere. Let them leave me alone for a spell."

The dark man turned, loosing his grip so that he might face her. His clear blue eyes stared down at her, enjoying her nakedness. And he smiled.

"There is no forgetting," he repeated, "nor any turning from the plan. But for now, let us try. We shall see what transpires here."

"Aye," murmured Raven, her hands moving to the fastenings of his clothing, tugging them loose. "Let us see."

Spellbinder sighed, looking down at the blonde head moving over his chest. Moving lower.

"Aye. So it goes."

Two

"The same moon that lights a lover's kiss may shadow
darker things. The wise man holds a lantern."

Ishkarian proverb.

The creature woke, if so precise a word may be applied to
a melding of corruption resulting in half-sensate awareness
of *being*.

Like an amoeba, or a germ, it was a thing of reaction
rather than direct application of thought. It had no purpose
of its own—not consciously—only that grim and bloody
reason for existence that was implanted in its protoplasm
by whatever force had brought it into life.

It became aware of its physical form. Of a body that
bore limbs on which it might walk, of arms with which it
might rend and tear. Of strength. It became aware of
vision, staring up at a sky that was blue-black, flecked
across with the silvery veins of distant stars, looming
clouds glistened by moon's light. It champed its teeth
together, grinding so that blood dribbled from its own lips
where the long fangs nipped flesh that was not flesh. It
heard the sound of the grinding and became, in conse-
quence, aware of aural sensibility. Of other sounds: dim
slurpings of waterlogged mud, the slow stir of fetid water,
the scampering of rats and other rodents, inhabitants of the
sewers and ditches.

It turned its head, encompassing in its new-found vision
the red eyes of a blunt-toothed creature that was sliding
towards it, saliva dripping from opened jaws in anticipation of rich feasting. A faint purring sound emanated from
the rodent's throat, transformed suddenly to a squeal of
terror as the creature swung an arm leftwards to grasp the
carrion-eater, too fast for the animal to escape.

Bones crunched as the massive fist closed on the body.
Mouth opened, exposing gleaming, scythe-like fangs that

glowed faintly in the dim light. Then the rodent was gone, the teeth gnawing, crunching on its flesh, the lips smacking in relish of the morsel.

The creature swallowed, savouring the taste of blood and warm animal fibre that awakened in what might be called its mind the memory of its purpose. It stood up. There was a sucking sound, as though a great chunk of mud and ordure was dragged loose from the sewer in which it lay. Had it possessed a sense of smell, it might have caught the midden-stink of its birthing place. But its senses were minimal, consisting only of those necessary to its immediate purpose: sight, hearing, faint vestiges of memory, and a lust for blood.

It licked the last traces of the rodent's life from its lips and peered around. It was in a ditch through which flowed a sluggish trickle of turgid water, oily in the moonlight from the decomposing rubbish floating on and under the surface. To either side of the water there rose up banks, steep and slippery with the outcastings of Haral's tenements. The banks were twice as tall as a tall man, but when the creature raised its arms, the talons tipping its seven fingers dug firmly into the soil atop the rim. It clenched its huge paws and began to bend its arms. Slowly, like some miasmic slug, it slithered upwards.

It reached the rim of the ditch and hauled itself over, resting for a moment on its belly as it attuned new-found senses to the new situation.

There was more light here, and it shook its head ponderously from side to side, letting its ears and eyes become accustomed to this new dimension. Lights burned in windows along the streets flanking the canal, and towards the centre of the city there was a greater glow that dimmed the moon; noise, too, coming from the streets and houses. The noise of voices and the stamp of animal hooves, of chinking goblets and clattering saddlery; the clash of blade on blade, and the shouts of men, the shrieks of women.

The creature moved towards the noise and the light.

To the west of Haral, where the city ended on the earthbound ocean of grass, a vast space was cropped and trodden down. A kli across, and three in length, the flat-

tened area was surrounded by pavilions and tents. Each
one shone bright in the glare of lanterns shaded against the
cool wind blowing from the estuary of the Horn river, a
wind that set the pennants and falchions mounted above
the gaily coloured canvas to fluttering. Crimson and green;
dark browns, akin to the heart-soil of Xandrone, glowed in
the lanterns' light; along with shades of blue, both pale as
summer skies and dark as Quwhon night; silver, too, and
gold, yellow, orange, flame. The flags and banners and
pennoncelles boasted designs that advertised or envied
their owners' ambitions and accomplishments. Here fluttered a Xand rampant, there a design of horn and sword;
another pennant carried a silver hoof on a background of
black, its neighbour, a horn-and-skull in gold on a leafed
sea of green; yet another bore simple lines, waving azure
on lines of brown and crimson so that the wind-driven
movement of the flag shook the eye, mesmerising the
vision.

These were the pennants of the Xand kings, the riders
and owners of the beasts. Beyond them lay the smaller
tents and lesser flags of the peripheral attendants of the
Summer Gatherings: the sellers of equipment and food; of
weaponry, swords and throwing stars, shields, knives,
bows, arrows of clean Ishkarian wood feathered with the
bright plumage of gitars and sullys. Also the tents of the
purveyors of gryllar and khif, of sweet Saran wine and
glara, s'ymstal and ba'ndath. Farther back still were darker
tents where necromancers spilled blood over bones to di-
vine the future from past deaths, or priests of the Stone
and the All Mother or the Lord Vedast sold prophecies and
absolutions in accordance with their consciences or avarice. And there, amongst them, were mingled the tents of
the dancing women.

These latter were brighter, setting a proud pattern over
the grim warnings of the priestly banners, like halcyons
over a sea of gloom. And from them, in counterpoint to
the wailing of the priests and the sombre beat of drums,
came the tinkle of cymbals and of fylar harps and the
laughter, like quicksilver, of women, the deeper roar of men.

But dominating all were the watchtowers of Haral's
judges.

Four there were, one set to either end of the central space, and two towards the centre, these latter spaced so that their lights and gaze should not be obscured by opposite movement. Six times as high as a tall man might reach his fingertips they stood, slim columns of wood standing on four heavy legs. For twice a man's height they were nothing but the legs and the ladders that climbed to the first platform, where lanterns were set and secondary judges waited to attest the decisions from above. Then another ladder, another platform, and finally a single, regal box, roofed over and equipped with sufficient space for a servant and wine and the torches of the judges.

These torches were comprised of seaweeds from the Dark Islands combined with grasses from Xandrone itself, and there were three colours.

Red signified a death; blue, a touch; and green a miss.

There were more complicated signals that were understood only by the judges themselves and their cohorts, or those riders and bettors involved enough in the contests to have extricated some kind of knowledge of the meanings of the complex signals of vari-coloured lights and fluttering hands. For the mass of the vast audience the three basic colours were enough. For most of them the roar and clash of battle, the bright flash of blood was enough. They had come to witness the thrill of the great contests, and the niceties of the rules—such few as existed—were merely a minor counterpoint to the overall excitement of combat.

In essence, the Xand combats were simple, and of four types.

First there was the te'enn contest. Essentially a demonstration of the breeders' wares designed to attract buyers, this was a straightforward race in which several Xands hauling carts loaded with stones pitted their strength against one another to haul the heavy, two-wheeled carts from one end of the combat ground to the other. The te'enna took place soon after sun's rise, and was attended mostly by purchasers and breeders.

Second, around mid-morning, came the te'kha competitions. Like the first races, these were tests of speed, though for individual animals. Poles high as a man's waist were set in lines along the length of the testing grounds, linked by ribbons of bright-dyed leather so that lanes were formed. Down these lanes rode the lightest of the Xand riders, urging their beasts on to massive effort in the attempt to win the prize of the gilded Xand skull awarded the swiftest animal. That and the extra rewards offered by the breeders.

Third came the te'zin. These were combats between individual Xands, bred solely for fighting. Attended by breeders and bettors, the te'zin combats occupied the whole of the central space, and had only one bloody ending. A breeder seeking to establish the supremacy of his strain might challenge another to pit his animal against the challenger's champion: the two beasts were released from either end of the grounds and the victor was the one left alive. The te'zin attracted a great deal of attention, both for the sight of blood and the chance of placing dalrs on the winning animal. For the breeders they represented a chance to establish a bloodline of fighting animals that would be watched—and later bought—by those clan chiefs or outland purchasers seeking animals of sound blood to establish a line of their own. From such stock had come the Kanthus boasted by the Inn of the Horns.

The te'zin fights occupied the central part of the day and the afternoon.

Then came the fourth and final part: the te'xanda.

This was the settlement of personal honours or clan feuds and it went on throughout the night, until the judges deemed the light too low for honest fighting.

There were two parts to the te'xanda—the Xand'il and the Xand'va. The former was a multiple combat in which feuding clans might put as many riders as they could muster into the arena. Armed with throwing stars, lances, swords, and spiked chains, the contestants fought until such time as one side was obviously victorious. It was a mêlée, in which death was dealt to anyone naked of the colours of the right side: which was the one with the most fighters alive in the end.

The Xand'va were personal combats.

Two riders appeared from either end of the grounds. Each man was armed in accordance with his personal wishes; one might carry a lance and a sword, the other a

set of throwing stars. The only thing forbidden was the
bow. They had the entire space of the combat grounds
open to them, and nothing was forbidden except arrows
and magic.

The Xand'va combats had only one outcome: death.

They attracted the largest audience of all the contests,
though the numbers of the actual fighters were low: at least
Xand'il combats afforded a rider the support of friends; the
Xand'va allowed no quarter, victory or death being the
sole outcome.

Raven and Spellbinder were watching one such combat.

They attended not from bloodlust, but from a desire to
study Xand fighters in action. During her time with Argor
and his outlaw band, Raven had learned to handle a Xand,
but the burly mercenary had deemed the massive beasts
too cumbersome for the kind of desert fighting he preferred and consequently relied mostly on horses. Similarly,
Spellbinder had only a passing acquaintance with the horned
beasts and sought to learn more of their usage in combat
by this firsthand experience.

The fight they were about to witness promised to be a
classic struggle, for both challengers were acknowledged
champions. One rider was from western Xandrone, a man
called Gall ta Kereth, who belonged to the Vanna clan
which herded under the shadows of the World's End mountains. He rode a huge, black Xand, its horns unadorned,
though dark about the points with the staining of old
blood. He carried a lance, a Xandronian scimitar, and a
chest-hung bandoleer of throwing stars. His opponent was
called Neval fet Griffin, a rider from the northern plains
where the Shima fed into the great bay fronting the Dark
Islands. He rode a Xand of grey and white, the horns
tipped with metal points, and carried a scimitar, lance and
bolas. He belonged to the Bar Klay clan.

The odds set upon the fighters were matched evenly.

It was the final combat of the day, timed to take place
soon after the evening meal.

Gall ta Kereth emerged from the western gates of the
field, Neval ta Griffin from the eastern. Both men sat on
their mounts in silence, waiting for the judges to end their
proclamations and signal the commencement of battle.

A trumpet sounded, its strident notes lingering long on the still night air.

Yellow torches blazed at either end of the tilting ground, then dropped simultaneously, sizzling into blackness. A gong belled.

Both riders urged their mounts forwards, drumming heels against shoulders and screaming encouragement. The Xands burst into a lumbering run that gathered speed faster than seemed possible for so massive an animal. The two men couched their lances beneath their right arms, settling the thick butts between ribs and biceps, letting the points droop to the horizontal position as they drew closer together.

The formal rules of the Xand'va demanded that each pair confine themselves to lances only in the first charge. Use of horns or throwing stars was forbidden on pain of execution. It was assumed that the lances would either end the fight or be broken on the shields carried by the riders. After the lance charge a man could use his stars or scimitar or bolas as he wished, or simply let his Xand kill his opponent.

Gall ta Kereth wore a round shield buckled to his left fore-arm; Neval fet Griffin carried a rectangular device. Both were convex in shape, so that the lance point would not glance off to strike the body, neither of which were armoured with anything more resilient than furs and strips of leather.

They came together like two juggernauts, or the meeting of storm clouds in a lowering sky. And like such meetings, bright sparks were struck, darting from metal as lance-tip met shield and burst fiery traces against the darkness of the torch-lit field.

Then they were past one another and fighting their Xands to a bellowing turn. Fet Griffin lay back in his saddle, a deep, dark score mark running from the centre of his shield to the upper rim. Ta Kereth was still upright, but a crack showed on the right side of his buckler.

They charged again, and this time the lances angled at those places weakened by the previous clash. Ta Kereth's struck the centre of the rectangular shield and splintered apart. Simultaneously, fet Griffin's lodged its point in the broken edge of his opponent's buckler and broke up as the galloping Xands thundered past one another.

A section of the eastern rider's weapon stayed firm in the split shield, but the force of the charge tore the remainder from his hand, spinning it up into the air. Ta Kereth's pole was reduced to a hand'span of wood, the larger section twirling high as though pursuing the other lance to continue the fight in the air.

The riders turned.

Fet Griffin dragged his bolas from the saddle and swung the cords about his head, using only his feet to guide his mount. Ta Kereth brought his shield up to guard his face and reached across his chest to pluck a throwing star from the bandoleer. He flung his arm out, releasing the star as the Xands closed again.

More sparks flew as the star glanced from fet Griffin's shield. Then a hurtling, whirling octopus of rope and metal tangled itself about the western rider's arms.

The Xandronian bolas was a simple weapon that required a great deal of skill to apply properly in combat. Comprised of three lengths of plaited leather, each one as long as a man's arm and connected at the epicentre to form a Y shape, the cords ended in spiked metal balls, like the heads of miniature morning stars. Used in close combat, the bolas could easily become a flail; used at long range it could trip an animal or entangle a man.

Ta Kereth was entangled.

His shield was wrapped to his chest, his right arm tied to his neck. The second star he had drawn was still clutched in the fingers of his right hand, but he was unable to free his arm to use the missile. Instead, he tried to sever the plaited leather with the razor edges.

But fet Griffin was closing in, drawing his blade.

The scimitar was long, curving on the down side to a slanting point afront a recurved topside that boasted a vicious hook, edged on both sides. Fet Griffin swung it as he closed on his opponent.

Ta Kereth swung sideways in his saddle, letting his Xand take up the fight as he fought to free himself. The animal sensed the urgency and danced its bulk away from the blow with a delicacy surprising in so large a beast. At the same time it ducked its great black head and gouged a horn along the flank of fet Griffin's beast. The grey Xand roared and swung its flanks clear of the darting ivory, seeking to turn it own head and drive a horn into the black one's bowels.

The riders parted.

Fet Griffin hefted his scimitar and charged again, seeking to press the advantage. Ta Kereth hacked at the bolas with the throwing star, letting his mount turn into the charge.

The two Xands met head on. Skull struck skull with such force that the repercussions were echoed over the combat-grounds. They staggered, falling apart, then began to spar with their horns like fencers seeking an opening.

Neither rider could touch the other. Fet Griffin was too far from ta Kereth to deliver a blow, and the western champion was still entangled in the bolas, struggling to sever the tough strands of plaited Xand leather.

Fet Griffin lowered his blade so as to use both hands to force his mount back. The Xand was unwilling to disengage, and while the great horns still clashed, ta Kereth succeeded in freeing his right arm.

His shield remained tight against his chest, impeding both his movements and his control of the black Xand, but he was now limber enough to hurl the second star. Fet Griffin saw the danger and heeled his mount forwards and to the side in an attempt to bring his blade within range before the Vanna clansman might cast the murderous bolide. The manouevre reduced the effectiveness of ta Kereth's missile so that it struck before it had full momentum. Fet Griffin deflected it easily with his shield, slashing across with his scimitar to gash a bloody line through the leather strips covering the westerner's left shoulder.

A blue torch flared from the box of the prime judge, indicating a wound.

Ta Kereth ducked beneath a second blow and fought his Xand round, running the animal away from his opponent. Neval fet Griffin bellowed a victory shout and plunged in pursuit.

"He must die now, surely," murmured Raven, the

excitement lending a touch of hoarseness to her voice. "What chance has he?"

"Judge not too soon." Spellbinder echoed the warnings of Argor. "Some men are not defeated until death claims them."

As though to prove his words, Gall ta Kereth flexed his shoulders, ignoring the crimson that the effort pulsed from his wound. Where fet Griffin's stroke had sliced flesh, it had also sliced the cords of the bolas, and now these strands parted, freeing the clansman's shield arm. Ta Kereth went on running, holding his shield close against his body as if still hampered by the bolas. A nervous whisper rose from those onlookers keen-eyed enough to spot the parting cords, near drowned by the roar of approval from the Bar-Klay clan and those watchers anticipating a kill.

Ta Kereth ran his Xand almost into the farthest confines of the fence surrounding the combat ground. Then swung his shield arm out to drag the beast's head round and parry fet Griffin's kill-stroke.

The apparent flight had lent the northerner sufficient confidence to anticipate an easy victory. He was charging his Xand full tilt, intending to crush the black animal against the fence and cut down ta Kereth from behind. Instead, he was abruptly confronted with a roaring, hooking head of mighty horns and a warrior with a scimitar cutting down at his body. His blade sparked noisy from the westerner's shield, and at the same time the black Xand drove a horn deep into the grey's flanks.

Fet Griffin's animal bellowed and lurched back. Ta Kereth's ripped a chunk of hide and flesh loose, and gouged again. The grey faltered, throwing fet Griffin off balance. He parried the Vanna man's downstroke and fought to bring his own scimitar into play. Ta Kereth leaned far over in his saddle and cut again. The northerner's blade dropped to the ground, his hand still firm upon the hilt.

A second blue torch flared.

Fet Griffin raised his shield defensively. Ta Kereth reached forwards, hooking the recurved edge of his scimitar against the rim of the buckler. Deftly, he twisted the blade, pulling back. The northerner was dragged sideways, his body suddenly exposed. Ta Kereth thrust forwards and up, driving the point of his sword into fet Griffin's shoulder. The shield fell useless as the arm dropped, tendons severed.

For an instant the two Xands parted. Fet Griffin's face could be seen, blanched pale by shock, the eyes wide as they stared helplessly at the Vanna man. Then ta Kereth ended it. There was a glint of torch light from the down-swinging scimitar, blotted out behind the darker cloud of crimson that spouted from the place where neck joined shoulder. Fet Griffin slumped in his saddle.

A red torch blazed, casting eerie light over the bleeding corpse. Then it was gone as the black Xand seized the moment of confusion to ram a horn deep through the grey's entrails and spill the beast on its side. The black reared, coming down with both forelimbs stiff, like battering rams, against the other's ribs. The grey screamed once and then was silent.

A roar erupted from the crowd, and money began to change hands.

Raven tugged her cloak about her body and began to push through the excited watchers alongside Spellbinder. The momentary fervour had left her now, replaced with a feeling of disgust. Death was no stranger to her, but this vicarious enjoyment of blood-letting, the placement of money on the outcome, rankled. She wondered how many of the audience, now eagerly debating the fight, would be willing to enter the arena themselves, how many would stake coin on their own weapon skills.

Sensing her sombre mood, the dark man settled an arm about her shoulders.

"Blood spilled for sport or gambling leaves a sour taste," he murmured. "Let's wash it clear with decent wine."

They walked back to the Inn of the Horns through the bright-lit streets, the milling celebrants, feeling curiously alien to the festive atmosphere.

The Inn was crowded, but Taram van Bril found them a table in a corner where a flask of Saran wine and a plate of titbits were brought them. The table was partially obscured by a pillar, thus affording a degree of privacy as they drank their wine.

"What now?" asked Raven. "Our purse has a bottom, and Haral's prices will soon reach there. Shall we seek employment, or move on?"

Spellbinder frowned, seeming lost in thought. When he replied, his voice was absent, as though her questions disturbed some concentration of the mind.

"I think we must stay awhile." He tilted the flask, filling their goblets. "There is something here . . ."

His voice tailed off and he closed his eyes a moment, concentrating.

"What is it?" Raven held her goblet untouched. "What do you sense?"

"Evil," he replied simply. "I cannot name it, but it is here."

Instinctively, the woman's hand dropped to the dirk sheathed at her waist. Her sword lay in the room above, packed with the remainder of her armour in the Yr leather satchel. She longed for the reassuring feel of the hilt, the familiar weight of the Tirwand blade: her companion's mood was reaching out to enfold her own senses. She shivered.

"This Black One of whom the Vedast-priest spoke?"

"Mayhap." Spellbinder shook his head as though to clear it of foggy thoughts. He raised his glass. "As I told you, there was something in that tale. Mayhap it concerns us."

Raven drained her goblet. "Why should it? Let Haral mind its own. And Kharwan, too. May we not walk our own path for a spell, free of the dealings of your sorcerer-priests?"

The warrior magician smiled slowly, sifting in his mind those words with which he might best convince the blonde woman of the inevitability of her destiny. To convince her without stirring her to anger, that was the problem; as ever.

"Do you remember the day we met?" He spoke carefully, gently; as one might speak to a loved companion whose will is strong and opinion at variance. "When you were merely Su'uan, a rescued slave?"

"And the bird saved me from the slavehounds, and you, with Argor, from the eunuchs of Karhsaam." Raven spoke dully, repeating a catechism grown tiresome with the telling. "Yes, I remember."

"The bird chose you," continued Spellbinder. "From the many it might have selected it chose you."

He leaned forwards on the table, staring at her eyes as he began to repeat the ancient prophecy.

"Doomed to suffer, doomed to conquer,
Knowing not the sacred tomes
Life and death, they both are hidden
In the chosen, infant frame.
New world born and old one dying,
Who to guess the godlike game?"

He paused, then spoke the other lines Raven had heard so many times before.

"Black its wings,
And black its soul.
Bird of night and bird of knowing,
Heed its call and heed its sowing.
Take the seed and let it grow,
All within your own soul growing."

"But there is no sign of the bird," she protested. "Scarce three times since we quit the Tribal Kingdoms have we seen it. Nor has there been any other sign: no augury, nor oracle to force us on some new path for All Mother knows what purpose."

"And yet there is something here," said Spellbinder doggedly. "And there is a feeling in my bones that we must stay. At least for a while."

"Kharwhan bones," muttered Raven, torn between bitterness and affection. "Some day you'll tell me of your birthing, if birthed you were rather than conjured by priest-kings' incantations."

As ever when questions of his origins arose, Spellbinder turned the conversation with an adroitness that was partly worked by wit and verbal deftness, and partly by some force of will that turned her attention from the subject.

As he emptied the wine flask into her goblet Raven had almost forgotten her attempt to probe his antecedents.

"Let's go to bed," he suggested. "We'll speak on this when the sun shines again."

Raven lay awake, staring at the moonlight that streamed in silvery beams through the shutters of the window. Beside her, a dark bulk in the dim room, was Spellbinder. A ray of pale light shone upon his hair, sheening the black with phosphorescent illumination. She studied his face, wondering.

They had ridden together some time now, and as she peered at the lean contours of his visage a smile formed upon her full lips. It was a smile of affection, of care, and yet it was tinged with curiosity and doubt at the same time. He was friend and lover, sword companion, guide, protector at times. Yet still a mystery.

His weaponskill was undoubted, proven in a myriad combats. He made no secret of his magical talents. She knew him better than any other living being. And yet she knew so little.

It was said by some that he came from Kharwhan, from the Ghost Isle; and he neither denied nor confirmed those rumours. She thought of the island, hidden behind its barrier of inviolable mist: home of the sorcerer-priests. Some there were who claimed the priest-kings to be demons, manipulating mankind for their own inscrutable purposes, malevolent dabblers in the affairs of humanity. Others thought them benevolent guardians, seeking only to aid the scattered nations ringing the Worldheart Ocean.

Once she had landed on the Ghost Isle, the mists parting to grant a berthing to the wolfboat she sailed. But then she had seen nothing of the mysterious inhabitants, receiving only a vision, an implanting of knowledge, from the strange tree that had sucked in her mind and sent her on yet another quest. That journeying had resulted in the death of a friend—the death of Silver—at Raven's own hand.

The memory soured her musings as might the lees of the wine spoil a glass drained too deep: she spat it out, concentrating on the present.

From the sands of the Southern Wastes, where first she

had met her companion, to the lands of the Altanate; to the great Rift of Ishkar and lonely, sea-lapped Kragg, domain of Gondar Lifebane, lord of the sea-reivers; to Quwhon's icy wastes and fabled cities; to the Tribal Kingdoms; all these roads had she travelled with Spellbinder. With him and the great black bird. And behind all that journeying, behind each happenstance of life that had started her feet along the individual paths, there seemed to exist some greater plan, some design too vast for her to comprehend.

Am I, she thought, *no more than a puppet, its strings pulled by forces invisible to my own eyes? Does Kharwhan control my destiny? Must I always obey the dictates of some power unknown to me? Unseen, but watching? Or can I choose for myself? Can I take up my sword and ride free, unhampered by ties or prophecies or auguries?*

A shadow hid the moonbeams for an instant and she turned with battle-honed instinct to glance at the window, one hand reaching for the gem-hilted sword beside the couch.

There was nothing there. No movement other than the play of cloud across the moon; no sound other than the gentle susurration of the nightbreeze through leaves and flowers.

But a prickling scratched at her scalp, a brief chill danced ghostly fingers down her spine.

Her hand closed on the hilt of the sword and the clean, straight blade hissed from the scabbard. She rose on cat's feet from the bed, moving to the window as silently as might a stalking panther, drifting wraith-like through the moonbeams to place herself in shadow, eyes turned outwards to survey the garden of the inn.

There was nothing.

Yet she knew there was *something*.

She paused, letting her eyes adjust to the different light that shadowed the garden. And saw.

Across from the window, where a fanciful watchtower— more ornament than guardpost—lifted its slender column from the rearward wall two red eyes returned her stare.

Crimson orbs afloat on a night-black sea they were. Implacable, demanding, unyielding. They watched her with unnatural calm, drawing her vision so that they came almost to hypnotising her, drawing out her concentration; quelling all doubts, all opposition to their fierce, unspoken, wordless gaze. Her blade dropped slowly to the floor, the point touching like a feather upon the boards.

Yes, said a voice in her mind. *Yes, you can leave it all. All you need do is die.*

But I did not wish for death. Her mind answered the other unspeaking voice silently. *Only for freedom.*

Is there such a thing? Does freedom really exist?

It must, she answered. *Surely it must.*

It was a question that was set against a question.

Why? Because you think it should? What is it? Tell of what you believe this thing is.

To ride free. Go where I wish, unencumbered.

Are you not encumbered by friendship? Would you leave Spellbinder?

No! Her mental reply was emphatic, a loud shout in her mind. She was surprised the dark warrior failed to wake. *I would not.*

He curtails your freedom, as must all loved ones. Would you give up your sword; your armour and your stars; the dirk and the sleeve-shield?

How could I? Anguish was a spectral echo through the corridors of her mind. *Without them I should become as I was before: a slave, defenceless.*

They too, then, encumber your choice, for you chose to learn such arts as were taught you.

Defiance welled fresh in Raven's mind: *Or go back into slavery! I had no choice.*

You might have become a free woman of Argor's band. You might have refused the swordskills.

And become a serving slut? What other choice was there? To go alone into the sands?

Yes.

I should have died. The heat or the hounds or some other slavetrain would have claimed me.

Yes, answered the silent voice. *But you might have died, and thus become free.*

What freedom is that? Raven demanded.

Perhaps the only one. Perhaps the only freedom is not to be born. A child is tied to its mother. A friend is tied to

*a friend. Habit links you to those things you know. There
are no islands, only projections of the mass. Are you ever
truly alone?*

She opened her mouth to say *Yes*, but realised she was
wrong. Instead, she answered: *Sometimes*.

But is that true freedom? asked the voice. *Or just your
excuse for it?*

*I don't know! By all the gods! how can I know? You talk
of freedom and then confuse my mind with tangles of
words. Must I be not born to find it? Or be born and then
die?*

Perhaps, said the voice. *Perhaps all of us must follow
the patterns; perhaps we have no choice at all.*

NO!

Her shout was vocal this time, a gusting of lungs and
windpipes that filled the room with an echo of sound.

A neighbouring guest slammed a fist against the wall.
Spellbinder awoke.

Raven stared out the window at the huge black bird
flapping its way across the sky like some dark portent of
storm. She slumped to her knees, tasting tears upon her
outthrust tongue. Then gave herself up to the dark man's
embrace.

Three

"In the gale's teeth the wise sailor will tack his vessels, else the elements destroy him."

Sea-reiver's warning

The creature feasted well that night, bloodlust driving it on long after its appetite was satisfied.

It ventured deeper into the city than the time before, spurred by some primeval compulsion, leaving behind a trail of carnage that was not fully realised until full light. Emboldened by its success, the thing wandered several kli into Haral, approaching close to the centre. There it found the lights and the noise and the crowds too threatening and drifted back into the shadows of the peripheral alleyways. It moved swiftly, and very quietly, its silent passage punctuated by the screams of the dying.

As night grew old and dawn threatened, it moved back towards the hiding place.

When the final tally was taken, it was discovered that eleven souls had gone to meet whichever gods they worshipped. And panic once again gripped Haral.

Dyn ta Kell called in all his men and set them to searching every empty building, each cellar and catacomb that might hide . . . anything: the Guardian could no more set a name on the slaughterer than he could describe it. He did what he could. Patrols checked the taverns and inns, attempting to establish some census of visitors. Sea-reivers from Kragg and tribesmen from the northern kingdoms were questioned in particular, for they were known at times to run amok. A difficult situation arose when ta Kell insisted on searching the Jedda's palace for fear the rumours of Beatsmen were accurate, in surmise that the humanoids had run amok. There were no Beastmen there, and the Jedda promised to lodge a formal protest. Neither the

Guardian nor the council were concerned: they sought only
to end the new horror.

Once more the celebration of the Summer Gathering
became dulled by fear.

It was less the fact of death than the manner and quantity in which it came. That and the unknown source. Men
died at each Gathering—some women, too—but they fell
to sword or knife, to bare hands or war-axe, from falls or
drowning or drink. The hideously mutilated corpses discovered by the patrols seemed to have fallen victim to
ravening beasts. Yet there was no sign of maddened animals within the confines of Haral's walls.

The creature slept through the day, its vestigial mind lit
by dim dreams of blood and soft, rending flesh.

It woke again as night clamped fear over the city.

It was hungry.

It moved forth, eyes alight with demonic glow. Stinking
saliva dripped from its mouth.

"Why?" Raven's voice was harsh with suppressed anger. "Why can we not leave now? Haral's Guardian has
men on every street corner, there are patrols throughout
the city. The clans have volunteered a hundred men to aid
them. Why must we stay?"

"Because," said Spellbinder.

"Because the bird appeared to me," interrupted the
woman. "Because the bird—or whoever speaks through
the bird—talked of freedom and duties and ties. I know no
one in this city. What friends we have are scattered over
the face of the world. If this night-stalker represents some
force sent against us, then surely it must be a favour to
Haral if we leave. If this thing is here because of us, then
our departure must draw it clear."

"It is not necessarily so simple," argued the dark man.
"The linkage is present, but the reason is dim."

"So we must stay now because we cannot understand
why we should?" Raven skewered a piece of meat and
began to chew irritably.

Spellbinder smiled. "I have told you what I sense. The
bird gave clear indication. I say we should stay."

"And I say we purchase horses and ride South." She

lifted her wine glass to her lips. "Uthak lies on the coast. We could ride there, or take a boat. Then on to Zantar and the Southern Cities. Perhaps Argor roams the Wastes again. At worst we might find employment for our swords."

"I thought you sought to avoid battle." Spellbinder said it softly, wrapping the cut with a smile. "If we're to fight in the Wastes, why not here?"

"It is not battle I avoid," shrugged Raven, "but puppet-pulling. I would be my own woman. I would ride where *I* wish, not follow pre-ordained tracks at the whim of some power I cannot understand."

"One more night," said the mage. "If no further sign comes to convince you, then we shall leave. A merchant-man departs on the noon tide, stopping at Uthak. We can find horses there."

"Until the morrow," agreed the blonde woman. "Then south."

She smiled at Spellbinder, glad that their companionship remained unbroken, yet wary of the easy manner with which he conceded her desires.

Separate to the concern evinced by Haral's council was the concern of the various officers of the religions followed by the city's inhabitants and guests. There were three main branches, and more minor worships than could be easily listed.

The chiefest were those of the Horn, the All-Mother, and the Stone. Of those, the priests of the Stone tended towards a philosophical indifference, claiming only a certain foreknowledge and the subscription of a way of life that was humanitarian rather than metaphysical. The adherents of the Mother took a pantheistic view that accepted the use of violence where necessary. The Horn priests, perhaps because they had most to lose, Xandrone being their only stronghold, were fervent in their advocacy of blood to answer blood.

That was the main reason they listened to the arguments put forward by the followers of the Lord Vedast.

After all, Vedast was a minor deity of the Horn religion, and so more acceptable than such alien monstrosities as the All-Mother or the Stone.

In essence—like most religions—they were similar in original concept. The differences of doctrine and practice had been introduced by the personal whims of the most forceful protagonists. But like swings to like as a lodestone swings to the polar apex, and Lord Vedast was listened to. At least in translation from his priests.

The Horn religion was basic: Xandrone existed on the profit of its herds and its grass. Thus the Horn God— whose true name was never spoken—was the father of all. His bride was Alaria of the Grass, the mother. From their union had sprung three sons: Gann of the waters, who brought rain and rivers; Karim of the soil; and Vedast of the seasons.

Gann and Vedast were dutiful sons, but Karim had felt a closeness to his mother that stemmed from his especial relationship of grass with soil. And sought, unnaturally, to usurp his father's place. The Horn God meted justice: Karim had died. The Horn God left the corpse of his son to fertilise the land of Xandrone, but the deistic conflict had produced in Vedast inklings of fear. A part of his supernal being had revolted against his father, finding, as Karim's rotting body decomposed, that the control of the seasons became more difficult. A part of Vedast's mind produced demons.

There had been poor harvests; storms; cold summers and over-long winters.

The priests of the Lord Vedast claimed to control the deity: to enjoy such communion that he would listen to their pleas.

Now they claimed control of the demon, of the night-slaughterer.

Vedast, they said, was angry. The people of Xandrone forgot him: he had chosen to remind them of his reality. They drifted from the old religion, leaving Horn God and minions for such upstart beliefs as the All-Mother and the Stone, even for Balan of the Knives or Kur the Knowing. Vedast had sent a messenger to bring the people of Xandrone back to the faith.

"But how," asked a priest of the Horn God, cognisant of the fact that nothing had actually been said against his own position, "do we placate this minor deity?"

"Guard your tongue first," replied the chief of the Vedast priests. "Then guard the strangers within our walls."

"But there are always strangers," answered the Horn priest. "They swell our coffers with outland gold each Summer Gathering."

"Most," said the Vedast-man evenly, "are honest travellers, come only to purchase our bounty. But some there are who represent a different thing: a thing alien to us, that might destroy us."

The Horn priest, pleased to hear that criticism was not levelled against him or his god, nodded and said, "Continue."

"Our city is full of unbelievers. Not all the citizens follow the old ways, but worse are the newcomers: seawolves from Kragg, traders from the Altanate, merchants from the Southern Cities, tribesmen, riff-raff. All bringing their own gods to vie with ours."

"Are you suggesting that these people have angered your Lord Vedast?"

The priest spread his hands, letting the movement of his body make clear the suggestion. There was a pause; a silence.

"Is your god so vengeful, then?" asked a Stone priest, cloaked in the dusty robes of Quell. "Would he make his anger so horridly obvious?"

"He is a vengeful god," replied the Vedast man. "His wrath is mighty."

"Why has he not struck at us?" enquired a priest dressed in blue robes, the eye of the Mother embroidered on the fabric. "Surely we should offend him more than some casual visitor?"

"Not so!" The Vedast priest swung around, bright eyes darting over the assembly. "He knows that you can tempt only those too weak to resist."

Someone chuckled, drawing a more furious glance from the speaker.

"There are others," he said, ominously. "Others with strange powers. Powers that threaten us all."

The Horn priest presiding over the meeting fought to assume command, to stem the rustling whisper of voices and louder cries of protest.

"Name names! Substantiate your claims."

"Easily," agreed the Vedast. "May I call a witness?"

The president of the gathering nodded, and the speaker shouted a name that was passed down the hall. As he waited for the outer doors to open he began to speak again.

"Three suns hence, two people came from a coastal vessel. Travellers from the Tribal Kingdoms. One was a woman, a blonde barbarian; the other a man, a dark man with magical strengths. Do you recall the writings in the Book of Vedast?" Before any could answer he spoke the words for them:

"One shall be black, the other fair,
They bring death.
Storm their coming, waste their going.
Death to all.
A man, a woman: unity,
Of death.
Beware the bringers."

There were protests from the gathered priests, mostly from those too urbane or worldly to accept so blank a prophecy. But acceptance over-rode disagreement.

And then the great doors opened and a short man shuffled in; tugging his robe about him as he glanced at the assembly seated on the benches ringing the hall. He was balding, a circlet of plaited leather holding back the thin strands of long hair that dangled from his temples, straggling over the greasy shoulders of his threadbare cloak.

The Horn priest motioned for the newcomer to speak.

"I am Taram, a priest of the Lord Vedast. I am honoured that so distinguished a gathering will grant me audience."

He shuffled round, bowing, until a priest shouted, "Speak." The president raised a hand and said, "Yes. Speak up, Taram."

The small man nodded and wiped a hand over his mouth, his eyes glinting with pleasure.

"Three days ago I met two outlanders." His voice was pitched higher than his body. "One was a woman. A fair woman, blonde of hair and visage, accompanied by a man. He was tall, with dark hair, dark as the woman's was fair."

"And this proves your prophecy?" The voice came from the rear of the hall. "Is this all you offer in evidence?"

"No!" The little priest swung round, aiming his voice and his red-eyed glare at the source of the interruption. "I offered them the protection of the Lord Vedast. They laughed at me, and then the dark one set a spell upon me, stilling my voice and movement until he was gone."

"Had I the same talent," someone said. But another shouted that he had seen it. And yet another that such magics were an offence.

"Do you claim these two to be the source of our trouble?" The Horn priest directed his question equally at the little man occupying the centre of the hall and at the chief of the Vedast priests. "Do you accuse them?"

"When I spoke of the Black One," shouted the small man, "they turned away, as though to avoid such questionings. They fulfill the dimensions of the prophecy, and the dark one was possessed of magical powers."

"I support the motion," said the senior priest. "We must question them."

"What motion?" shouted a Stone priest. "All we have heard is hearsay."

"We shall question them," announced the president. "I have heard sufficient that I am convinced of the need to investigate."

There was a vocal difference of opinion, some priests crying that this represented victimisation, others that it was an affront to freedom. But the vote was carried on a wave of fear: it was agreed that representation be made to the council for the apprehension and questioning of two outlanders, one a dark-haired man, the other a blonde woman.

A delegation attended the council, and that body—with little else on which to base its investigations—listened. A search was instituted for the strangers answering the Vedast priest's description.

The creature slaked its lust in fresh blood. More this time than ever before. It felt hungrier, stronger with each fresh killing. It took less time now, as though its dim mind sensed the nearing of its unknown purpose and hurried to build the trail of bloody ruin that would lead to culmination.

Rather than savour its prey, it simply killed and moved on. Moved through the alleys of Haral to the wider streets between waterfront and centre. It even ventured into one wide, well-lit avenue, flitting between the trees lining the arcade until a patrol caught sight and gave pursuit.

Then it ran.

It ran towards the centre of Haral, almost as though it sought to lead the Guardian's men on a deliberate path.

It ran towards the Plaza of the Horns, then turned into a side alley, the patrol in close pursuit.

The alley ended in a small square. The blank faces of private buildings covered three sides, their windows and doors shuttered against the terror. The fourth side was occupied by the gate of the Inn of the Horns.

The creature scaled the gate. And by the time the patrol found entrance, it was gone.

The guards posted inside the wall were both dead. One lacked a skull, the other a chest. Three guests were slaughtered in similar bloody fashion. And the crimson spoor marks left by the thing led to the rear of the building. It was the first time it had left such tracks, and it was as though it wished to leave a trail; as though it deliberately paddled in the blood of its victims.

The spoor went through the stables, where two Xands lay dying. Then out to the garden beyond, up the wall of the overhung porch, and up towards a window at the hindside of the inn.

Five men waited in the grounds with crossbows and spears at the ready. Five more went to the front to enquire who occupied the room indicated by the bloody tracks.

"Why," said Taram van Bril innocently, "two outlanders. A fair woman known as Raven and a dark man called Spellbinder."

Four

"To view the ultimate truth does not necessarily lead
to enlightenment. At times the path goes down into
madness."

The Books of Kharwhan.

"You are damned by the evidence. You cannot deny it."

"I can and do. You have no evidence."

"Outland magic? A trail of blood? Is that not evidence?"

"I know not what you say. Whose blood?"

"The blood of slaughtered innocents, despoiled in pursuit of your foul designs."

"I have no design other than to leave this place. I have spilled no blood here."

"No? Why, then, do the funeral pyres call all Haral to the mourning?"

"Am I chosen as scapegoat for that you cannot comprehend? Do you lay the blame on that target easiest for your accusations?"

The priest gestured at a soldier, who stepped forward to lash a flail against Raven's back. The three lengths of plaited hide brought a fresh welling of blood from her already broken skin, the thin rivulets of crimson running down from the cut, crossing the earlier marks to trace a path over her naked buttocks and dribble sluggishly around the curves of her thighs.

She ground her teeth together, determined that no sound should escape her lips in indication of weakness. But she was unable to prevent the tears coursing from her eyes, or the instinctive flinching of her naked body.

The priest stared at her for a while, allowing his gaze to travel down the contours of her flanks and legs. He folded his hands inside his robe and turned away, letting his gaze travel to the brazier at one side of the cell, where irons began to glow in the hot coals. He nodded for the soldier to stand back, and paced slowly over to where the satchel containing her armour and sword was dropped on the bare stones.

He lifted the sack.

"You bear a slave brand on your thigh, yet carry armour and weaponry befitting a champion."

"Given me," snarled Raven.

"And the creature came to your room." The priest continued as though she had not spoken. "Pursued, it ran to you."

"It appeared at the window. I drew blade to slay it."

"It came to you. And your companion. Who works magic."

"Would that he could magic you to whatever cesspit spawned you."

"So you affirm his evil talents. That is a step on the path to truth."

"Free me! Hand me my blade, and I'll send you there myself."

"Belligerent." The priest's voice was deceptively gentle, almost caressing. "There will obviously be much application of pain needed in your case, before we may extract the truth from you."

"I have told you the truth. I know nothing of this beast you fear so much. Nothing."

"A claim I do not believe. I shall leave you alone for a time. Think on your story and your guilt. When I return, I shall question you again. When I do, the incorrect answers will not bring the flail, but the irons. Think on that."

The door thudded shut behind her and the torches dimmed. Only one remained alight, casting a faint, flickering glow across the cell. She turned her head, wiping away the tears on her uplifted forearm, trying to attain a more comfortable position despite the chains. They linked her wrists together, holding her arms up above her head where they were fastened to the stanchion of the great stone pillar set in the centre of the cold, shiny room. Manacles ringed her ankles, bolted to the stone so that she could not properly stand upright, but must constantly support her weight upon her arms.

She could feel the slow turgidness of blood upon her thighs, on her back the sting of the flail. Something moved behind her; a dry, rustling sound. Then tiny teeth nibbled at her ankle: she was unable to kick the creature—whatever it might be—from her. It gnashed its teeth and lifted cool paws against her calf. She shuddered as little claws dug into her skin and the creature began to climb her leg. Then groaned as it began to lick the blood from her thigh, moving steadily higher, towards the wounds on her back.

Spellbinder could see his torturers, for he was stretched out on a wooden table facing a lantern that hung directly above his eyes. His wrists were fettered to a kind of roller built into the top of the table; his ankles were chained to bolts set through the bottom.

Each time he angered his questioner a soldier turned the roller a fraction more, dragging the victim's hands farther and farther away from his shoulders.

Sweat glistened on the dark man's face and his blue eyes burned with concentration.

"You cannot deny it," said the priest. "Your companion has admitted you a sorcerer."

"I know nothing of this beast." The dark man's voice was husky with pain and the effort of speaking. "Why it came to us, I cannot say."

The handle turned; the roller drew round: the body stretched.

"I do not believe you."

"I cannot help what you believe. I can only tell you the truth: it is up to you to choose between reality and what you want to hear."

"No. It is up to you to tell me what I want to hear, or listen to your own screams."

The handle turned again.

Spellbinder's chest heaved with the effort of containing his body in a single piece. He could smell the fetid breath of the priest in his nostrils. Smell, too, his own sweat. He closed his eyes, forming a spell that would sunder the chains.

Nothing happened.

The rack drew tighter: he could feel the sockets of his shoulders begin to tug clear; feel the constraint of flattened lungs turn his breathing to a hoarse rasp; feel his hips and knees and ankles begin to expand.

He chose another path.

The only path left.

"I will tell you." He emphasised the hoarseness of his voice, letting it grow weak. "Ease this pain and I shall tell you."

The priest smiled, nodding at the soldier. The roller spun back upon itself: the pain lessened.

"The truth," said the priest. "Only the truth, else we begin again."

Why this magic had failed him he could not understand. Perhaps it was some part of a greater plan; a necessary part, he hoped, for it was resulting in a great deal of suffering. But it was no longer there, so there was a need for some alternative: if this went on, he and Raven would be dead.

"The creature is connected to us." He chose his words as carefully as a Karhsaam fencer might choose his blows: to convince the priest and leave open an avenue of escape. "I am not sure how, but it is. I am a mage of some skill. Raven is a swordsmistress. We came here for no other purpose than to enjoy the Gathering; it seems we attracted the beast."

"This is not an answer." The priest's face twisted as abruptly as the lever of the rack turned. "The truth, I said."

Spellbinder screamed. The shriek was not entirely false.

"We brought it! It is summoned by Raven! Loose me and I'll tell you how to trap it."

The rack eased. The dark man licked blood from his lips, letting his mind sort the next words so as to make them convincing.

"Tell me," smiled the priest. "This time the truth."

"You must set us alone in the combat grounds. Set soldiers about the fence, but no others. We must have with us our armour and swords." The priest snorted derision, prompting Spellbinder to add, "Arm your men with bows. Bring priests, too. Set the arena round with fire. The thing will come then."

"Why should I believe you?" asked the priest. "Perhaps you seek only to escape."

"Ringed round with archers? Lit by fire? How could we?"

The priest pondered it for a moment, then:

"Very well. When must we do it?"

"The next dark night. The last night. Clear the arena first, then bring us there. Until that time you must leave us together."

"To conjure some new magic?" demanded the priest. "To escape us?"

"Had I magic to escape you," said Spellbinder honestly, "I should have used it ere now. I cannot. But set guards around the cell if you will."

"I shall," said the priest. "Doubt not that I shall."

They were put together in a dungeon built into the lowest part of the Horn Temple's basements. There were no windows for they were too deep beneath the ground. There was no light, and the only exit was a narrow tunnel that forced them on to hands and knees for the entering, and was sealed by a solid slab of stone without window or chink.

For three turnings of the sun—by Spellbinder's estimate—they remained in darkness, seeing light only twice a day when food was brought them. It was poor food, near as miserable as the cold stone floor over which washed the seepage of the temple's drains. There was no covering to the flags, no straw nor blanket to fight the chill. Their only covering was each other and the tiny, scuttering animals that joined them.

"What profit do we gain from this?" Raven clutched Spellbinder to her body, welcoming his warmth. "They will shoot us down."

"Perhaps not." The dark man's teeth chattered as he spoke, the cold seeping deep into his tortured bones. "We may yet fight free."

"From out a ring of archers? Your magic has deserted you, and even our swordskills cannot defeat a phalanx of bowmen."

"Something may come," avowed the mage, powerless, "we may yet escape."

"The creature may come," muttered the woman, "but what then?"

"I know not. It was all I could do to free us both from torture, beyond that I have no knowledge."

"Nor magic, either." For the first time a note of fear crept into Raven's voice. "Why is that, think you?"

"Mayhap the priests of the Horn God or the Lord Vedast weave some greater magic." His voice evinced more doubt than Raven could ever recall hearing there. "Mayhap we were destined to stay."

"So we come back to paths and plans again. And to the absence of choice."

"I do not know." His voice grew anguished now, confusion and regret mingling. "I know only that I am robbed of my powers and our only hope of escape is to follow the plan I set out."

"And face this creature in the arena." Raven was doubtful. "If it comes."

"If it does not," grunted Spellbinder, "then our innocence must be proven."

"Will the priests accept that?" Raven asked. "Or kill us for betraying them?"

"If the latter," said the mage, "then at least we die under the open sky. That is better than down here in the darkness."

"Aye." Raven stroked his hair, instantly regretting her doubts. "That will be better."

They were taken out from the cell by armed guards, whose torches blinded their light-starved eyes and whose rough handling bruised their torn bodies. They were given a small chamber in which to cleanse themselves and dress in their own armour.

Then, weaponless, they were ushered through the long corridors of the Horn Temple, up winding flights of narrow stairs, through indifferent, silent rooms, to a hall where the priests waited.

Mostly they were adherents of the Horn God or the Lord Vedast, but amongst them stood followers of the All-Mother and the Stone, robes of dusty brown and ocean's blue contrasting with the scarlet and ochre of the presiding cantors. They shifted back as the two accused entered the room, a murmuring of prayer filling the hall with susurrant echoes. Several shook emblems of their faiths in the direction of Raven and Spellbinder, but more stared with angry eyes and hostile words.

The light was brighter here so that the two on trial blinked and sought to avert their gaze from the brilliance, which gave the priests reason to assume their guilt, feeling that it was the sight of censers and symbols that prompted the aversion.

"Take them to the fields," cried the chief of all the Horn priests. "Now, and swiftly. Let us settle this thing."

There was a murmur of agreement, and rough hands shoved the two companions in the direction of the carved metal doors.

Outside, in a small courtyard that was paved with beaten copper, there waited a closed carriage. The wheels were huge discs of blackened wood, one mounted either side of the narrow platform, leaving scarce enough space for them to stand upright. Rods of metal formed a cage that was fixed to the floor of the cart, the roof and sides draped with black cloth. A gigantic Xand, its horns the same midnight colour as its hide, stood between the traces.

Raven and Spellbinder were lifted bodily into the cage. The door slammed shut with a grating of keys, and the black cloth fell down over the opening, shutting out all light.

The cart rumbled forwards.

The priesthood had agreed with the council that the event should be kept as quiet as was possible. That no official announcement be made, nor any of the public admitted to the combat grounds during the test—only a few had the gall to call it a trial. Which meant that most of Haral knew something was going on, and that it had to do with the demon, but only a select few knew exactly what.

Rumour had it that the creature was taken and scheduled for execution at the darkest hour, when its black soul would go back to whatever hell it came from . . .

That a secret sacrifice was to be made, the victim a highborn virgin . . .

That an outland magician had confessed to conjuring a spirit from one of the seven pits and was now to meet his end at the priests' hands . . .

That the priests of the Horn God had challenged the demon and would meet the thing in supernatural combat . . .

The rumours were vague, unsupported by clear evidence, but they remained strong enough to attract the larger part of Haral's citizenry, both resident and transient, to attend the event. It became necessary for the priestly procession to wait within the confines of the Horn Temple until sufficient force of the Guardian's men could be sent for to escort them through the streets.

A phalanx of spearmen opened a way, and then more flanked the swaying cart, surrounding the black-shrouded vehicle and the suddenly-nervous priests with the same protective blanket of metal. Their progress was slow, for it was necessary to force a way through the crowds as a man might wade through the thick, clinging grass of the Xand plains, at the same time protecting their sides and rear against the anger and excitement of the watchers.

At the combat grounds the crowd was blocked, held back by the full weight of the Guardian's soldiery. Barriers had been erected, patrolled by armoured men, and entry was forbidden on pain of death or heavy fining. Even so, there were some who slipped through to witness the event.

The great field was reduced in size, movable fences being erected about the centre of the tilting grounds so that the focus of attention was at the median point. Tall poles, each one carrying a great torch of oil-soaked material or a brazier of pitch at the top, were set at intervals along the fence. Between each pole stood an archer, his cross-bow nocked and aimed inwards. The fence itself was near high as a man, so that the quarrels of the bows formed a kind of spiky barrier atop the woodwork.

Raven and Spellbinder were brought up to the edge of the fence and dragged from the cart. Without ceremony, but with much fear, they were thrust in through a little gate that was afterwards fastened with a massive lock.

Then their weapons were tossed over the fence.

"What now?" asked Raven as she buckled her sword about her hips. "We are trapped securely as before."

"Wait." Spellbinder seemed more confident now that he was free of the dungeon. "Wait and watch."

With no other choice, Raven settled to checking her armour. The mail shirt of fine-wrought black links went some little way to reassuring her waning confidence, as did the sleeve-shield buckled to her left fore-arm. The belt of throwing stars encircled her waist with the conforming tightness of an embrace, and the familiar tug of the silver-bladed sword lifted her spirits as she hefted the blade in the smoking air.

Beside her, Spellbinder was accoutred in his black cuirass, his blade of Quwhon steel at his side, a gleaming silver shield upon his left arm.

He smiled as he turned to face her.

"My powers return. Some force still binds me, but I grow stronger as I speak."

"Strong enough in your magicking to take us from here?" demanded Raven.

"Not yet, but soon." He touched her cheek, tenderly. "Until then, trust in your blade."

Raven glanced at the fence. Above the upper level, like miniature turrets, stood the helmets of the Guardian's men, between each pair of helmets there glinted the polished head of a cross-bow bolt. She wondered what use a blade might be against the volley of those metal shafts and glanced, instinctively, at the sky. Half-heartedly, she hoped the bird might be there, come back to aid her as it had done so often before. But there was no sign of the dark messenger, no sign of anything but impending death.

Beside her, Spellbinder touched a clenched fist to his forehead, eyes blank with concentration.

"Something stirs," he murmured. "I feel it."

"What?" Raven turned, scanning the arena, sword in hand. "What is it?"

"I cannot tell, not yet." Spellbinder appeared confused. "I sense evil, but formless, mindless. I must concentrate."

The creature slunk silently through the darkness.

There were fewer lights now, less people in the streets. And those it saw, it avoided—it had a new purpose this night. A dim part of its mind told it that a part of its task was completed, a chain of events set in motion that would lead to the culmination of the overall plan. Now one more task lay ahead; the last. It did not formulate the thought in so ordered a manner, for it did not, in the proper sense, *think*. Rather, it was prodded by some external influence

that allied with its bloodlust to direct it. What it knew was
that it must venture through the city to the place beyond
where it would fulfill its role and reap its reward.

It drifted like a wraith through the streets until the sound
of voices and the brilliance of torches halted it.

The beast paused, slinking around the edge of the crowd.
The tempting presence of so much succulent flesh brought
saliva to its mouth and set it to grinding its fangs together.
But the presence of something else, stronger now than ever,
caused it to ignore the feast set out before it, drove it on.

It moved westwards, circling until it reached a darker
area, devoid of people. A tower stood there, a single torch
burning at the apex. Beyond was a fence, a field, and then
a knot of people. They all looked inwards, to where a
second fence was built up, topped by smoking light and
ringed by armed men. The creature knew without understanding how or why, that the one it sought was at the
centre of that ring. It moved forwards.

The majority of the onlookers were held back to the
southern and eastern sections of the combat grounds, penned
there by the guards and their own fear. These places,
closest to the city, felt safer than the darkness of the farther
extremities. Even so, there were a few who had managed
to slip through the ring of soldiers and now clustered about
the central arena, waiting.

Their waiting ended in bloody horror.

There was a scream, and a body, gutted like a fish,
tumbled through the air. Blood spattered the startled faces
lifted to follow the ghastly passage. Then a massive, stinking juggernaut ploughed through the crowd. Men and a
few women went down beneath scything claws, clubbing
arms. Taloned feet crushed the fallen, and fanged jaws
rent flesh, crunched bone.

The guards turned, unleashing spears and cross-bow
shafts against the invader. They were useless: those mis-
siles not struck aside by the wind-milling arms penetrated
the body of the creature and hung there, unheeded. It was
as though its form was simultaneously solid and formless.
As though no organs existed within its huge frame that
might be pierced by steel. It was unkillable, unstoppable.

It carved a blood-drenched path to the fence and paused. The arms swung forwards, gripping the wood; heaved back. The fence broke, great chunks of timber tearing loose like matchwood smashed by an angry child. Two torch poles crashed down in showers of sparks. The on-lookers fled.

Raven and Spellbinder faced the monster as it came through the shattered fence.

Illuminated in the torch-light, it was gigantic, a great black shadow that snarled and roared, baring glistening fangs and flexing claws that glowed with a wavering phosphorescence and the sheen of fresh-spilled blood.

Raven sprang forwards, swinging the Tirwand blade at the creature's belly.

Spellbinder shouted, "No!"

But it was too late. The blow landed, cutting deep through the substance of the thing's midriff. Raven twisted the sword, withdrawing to cut again.

The second blow failed to land, for the thing caught the sword in one huge paw and dragged it from the woman's grip as casually as if the razor edge were a straw. Spellbinder darted in, cutting at the eyes. The monster flung one arm out, smashing the dark man back off balance.

Battle skill alone kept Spellbinder on his feet, though he staggered under the force of that blow, and barely lifted his shield in time to deflect the second swing. Red sparks danced from the face of his buckler as the claws grated over the metal, leaving behind a row of gouge marks that no sword might have set there. Raven sprang to her companion's aid, unleashing a star with hate-spawned force, hurling a second even before the first had landed.

The first struck the creature in the shoulder, digging deep. The second hit the face, carving into the cheek, silver against blackness.

The thing paused, scratching at its face to pluck the missile loose. A sluggish pulsing of red ichor welled from the gash. The star fell to the ground. The monster paced towards Raven.

She saw her blade, silver edge stained with the ichor, on the grass and dived towards it. Caught it up, rolling.

Came to her feet with Tirwand steel carving air before her. Cut again at the beast. And again saw the blade sink deep with no effect. Again she cut. A third time, a fourth.

"Stand clear!" Spellbinder's shout held fear; not for himself, but for her. "Raven, beware!"

The warrior-magician rose behind the creature, hefting his own dark blade. He lifted the Quwhon steel two-handed. Brought it down in a whistling, sundering arc that dug it deep between neck and shoulder. Simultaneously, attuned to Spellbinder's style of combat, Raven thrust in again, ignoring his warning. She drove her own sword into the thing's belly, setting all her strength and weight behind the thrust. The beast paused. From its chest there extended the tip of Spellbinder's sword; from its back, Raven's blade struck out half an arm's length, all dripping and foul. It turned, fixing red eyes on the mage. Raven felt its power then, for its turning threatened to loose her grip on the gem-hilted sabre. She twisted the blade and drew it loose. Spellbinder did the same.

By every law of nature the thing should have fallen then. Its belly was slit open; its heart—if heart it possessed—was cut through; its upper body was riven from shoulder to breastbone. It roared and sprang at Spellbinder.

The dark man raised his shield and cut at the paws reaching towards him. He struck fast, black blade darting swift as summer lightning. The paws should have fallen from the stump-like wrists, severed by that awful stroke. They did not. Instead, one took the blade and grasped it and tore it free of the sorcerer's grip. The other struck the shield, turning the silver, claw-scarred surface aside as easily as a man might bat away a troublesome fly. Then the creature dropped the Quwhon blade and set its paws about Spellbinder's waist, lifting him.

The warrior-magician groaned with the pain of the grip and drew his dagger, slashing at the wrists. Raven moved in behind the monster, slashing her own blade at its back, its head, its legs.

She sought some vulnerable spot: probed into the back to where the lungs should be; hacked at the spine until the flesh lay open over the same dark nothingness as covered the exterior; dug at the testicles; sought to hamstring the beast.

Uselessly. It hurled Spellbinder from it, tossing the dark man's body as casually as a child tosses aside a discarded toy.

"Raven, flee!"

Spellbinder's voice rose above the roaring of the monster, above the shouting of the soldiers, above the *twang* and *whir* of the cross-bows. Then he struck the fence and was silent, a crumpled shape draped over the wreckage of timbers strong enough to pen a Xand.

The thing turned towards Raven.

For an instant she stared at it. Saw the spears and the bolts and cuts that decorated its body like obscene medals. Then it was on her. She hacked at it with her sword, drove the sleeve-shield into its face and throat and bowels.

Then screamed as it grasped her and dragged her towards its awful imageless face. Fetid breath gusted sewer-stink at her nostrils. The ichor that splattered her hands and face as she cut about its head burned her and nause-ated her.

The beast laughed, and from its gaping mouth came a voice.

"Now you are mine."

The voice was soft, like a gentle breeze over summer grass, smooth as caressing silk on a naked body. And evil. Somehow the very softness of it, the gentle, silkiness of its quality made it more evil. Worse than Belthis' dry rustle or the throatiness of the Frozen God. Worse than any vileness she had heard.

"Come to me."

She drove the point of her shield into the creature's temple. Saw ichor flood from the wound that should have pierced the brain and dropped it instantly.

But there came only red fire that wrapped about her and choked her breathing so that she gasped and fought for life and sanity and escape.

And then there was nothing.

Five

"To hold a firm belief is to hold a firm character. The fact
of holding does not, necessarily, justify the original belief."
                                    The Books of Kharwhan.

It was dark and cool and damp.

There was no sound other than the slow, laboured gasps
of lungs in pain. Fighting for air. No movement other than
the faint twisting of tortured bones, raw skin. No feeling,
either, except that of pain and wetness, and the chill that
trembled the tortured body.

I am alive. I can feel, so I must be alive.

Eyes opened: a painful movement: darkness.

A hand twisted: pain. And constraint.

The same with the other hand. The feet, too.

So: imprisonment.

But where?

Somewhere cold. Somewhere wet. Somewhere alone.

Why?

Not death, which was expected. Nor life, it seemed.

What?

Limbo? Some magical prison? Some place between the
worlds?

A faint flash of glimmering lightning gave Spellbinder
the answer, and with it the memories . . .

He had thought to die when the beast tossed him so
casually through the fence of Haral's combat grounds. He
might have died, but for his armour and whatever power
guarded him . . .

The lightning reminded him of the creature's claws.
Phosphorescent, glinting, darting . . .

Raven!

No. She was gone: he was alone . . . Alone on the
sea . . .

Full memory came back.

61

The creature had taken Raven. It had fought them both; them and Haral's soldiers. Taken Raven after leaving him for dead like a carcass hung on a fence. It had disappeared in fire. Gone.

The priests had taken him down from the fence and tended his wounds: repayment for the false words spoken under torture. Then they had announced him outcast . . . lashed him to a section of timber.

Abruptly, with the same sudden clarity that had awoken his mind, he remembered exactly where he was, what had happened.

They had decided against killing him: in a way, his tortured promise had come true. The beast had come—and gone. So they had chosen not to execute him. At least, not themselves. Instead, they had lashed him to a platform of timber and taken him out beyond the Dark Islands to the open sea.

Then cast him loose.

He was afloat now; afloat on the empty sea of Worldheart with his wrists and ankles tied down to the timbers he rested on. In time, those timbers would become waterlogged. And sink. Or thirst would dry his body to a salty husk; unless some sea creature ate it first.

He strained against the ropes and tried to fashion a spell, a simple one: to bring fresh water to his salt-caked mouth.

Nothing happened; nothing at all. It was as before, back in the dungeons of Haral when his magic failed him and he had only his wits on which to rely.

He was alone. Totally. More than ever before.

"Very well," he mouthed, for he could not properly shape coherent words, "so it goes."

He rested back against the salty planks of his tiny raft, staring up at the star-flecked sky. He ignored the pain of the ropes and the cuts on his body that were licked by the tongues of salt washing over his miniscule platform, and concentrated only on the movement.

It was a gentle movement, soporific and lulling, sleepy; like a cradle. The waves splashed over him, the barrier formed by his raft causing the swell to break and fleck him with foam, but it became, after a while, a soft licking of numb fluid. He slept.

Brightness and heat woke him, dragging him relent-
lessly up from his self-induced rest to feel again the agony
of salt on open wounds, the pain of rope-burned limbs
exposed to a burning sun. When he opened his eyes the
brightness drove shafts of pain deep inside his skull. His
ears ached and his nostrils burned; his mouth was a dry,
parched opening through which breath and water came in
equally painful measure.

Perhaps I shall die, he thought. *Perhaps they have left
me alone. Perhaps they want me to die.*

And with that thought came a flood of rebellion, naked
and raw as the new-born infant's protestation against its
birth, the severence from dark womb into bright life.

"No!" he screamed, forcing the word past sticky, sun-
dried lips. "No! I will not die. I cannot! Must not! Not
yet. Not until I find Raven again."

The effort drained him and he fell back against the
timbers, dark hair spreading out over the edge of the raft to
dribble in the gently-rolling ocean, where fishes rose to the
surface to nibble at the strands and glide away, disappoint-
ed by the tastelessness of the morsels.

Three times during that day huge sea-beasts surfaced
close to the raft. One was a creature of tentacles and eyes
and hooked mouth set round with horny ridges of bone;
another was fleet, smooth of body and grinning mouth, in
which shone rows of massive, curved teeth; the third was
all neck and mouth and muscle, its body never leaving the
deeper water as its head studied the titbit stretched on the
raft; its jaws might have swallowed up man and wood
together in a single gulp.

But none touched him.

And in the night a saviour came.

At first he was aware only of a weight upon him, and
sought to twist his body so as to disturb the sea-thing he
believed was readying to devour him. Instead of shifting,
the thing dug claws against his armour and hawked a
strident cry.

He woke and saw the bird perched upon his chest.

Raven? he asked, not using words. *Where is she?*

There was no answer.

Am I to die, then? I might accept it better if I knew why. Surely I am owed that.

The bird lifted a taloned foot towards the ropes binding his wrist, the right one. It tugged at them: they parted as though cut by Tirwand steel. It trod over his chest to the left side; parted the ropes there. He sat up, clutching at the sides of the raft to support himself. His movement set the fragile vessel to rocking, threatening to tip it, hindside up, into the ocean. The bird flapped its wings and lifted into the sky. Only when the rocking had ceased and the raft was still again did it return to unfasten his legs.

And then a voice came inside his mind, one he knew.

The bird will save you. You are not alone, nor ever have been. Trust. As you ask the one called Raven to trust you, so trust now. That way you may find help. Trust.

He voiced mindless assent, too weakened by pain and water and wind to do otherwise.

Abruptly, swift as a lizard's tongue catches the unwary fly, he was powerful again. It was as though the tortures of the Horn Temple were forgotten. As though the wounds sustained in the arena had never happened. As if the long klis of salty ocean were behind him. And better—better by far—was the return of his magical strength. Like bright sun after gloomy night the power dawned again. Like spring rain on winter fields, summer on growing shoots. It came back.

And like a man new-come from sickness, he tested his strength.

He turned a patch of ocean to boiling water, then quelled the steam with a fall of snow. He shaped a spell that would grant him a picture of Raven; but none came.

Not that, said the voice. *That must wait.*

What then? he replied in the same wordless language. *What must I do?*

Trust the bird. Only that. Trust as you ask others to trust it.

Very well, he agreed. *But I shall want answers in time.*

They are given, said the voice, *when the right questions are put. Sometimes.*

Chastened, Spellbinder bowed his head. He sank to his

knees, bracing his arms against the rocking of the raft; and waited.

A shadow fell over him. He felt the beat of wings loud on the bright air. He felt himself diminished, become smaller. The wings' wind buffeted him; the riplets of the swelling ocean became mighty waves. The raft became a great floating platform across which he might have walked for half the sun's turning.

There was a shadow blocking out the sun, and then he was lifted in massive talons as gentle as a mother's hand upon her child. Lifted up, aloft; like a bird, or an ear of corn grasped by a bird.

He flew. Flew over the waves, leaving the raft behind. Flew over black-sailed wolf-boats and bright-painted galleys. Flew over storm and calm; over islands lost in the wastes of Worldheart and men lost in their own ambitions.

It was a flight without time and it took him to the edges of the mist that hid the Ghost Isle, Kharwhan, from curious gaze.

The bird passed over the mist, entering a clear, bright bay that made the mist appear like a reef sheltering some idyllic island.

Beyond the mist was a ring of bright water, blue as the fairest, most perfect topaz. No waves disturbed the placid shore, merely a gentle lapping of bluest water on bright silver sand. Beyond the sand lay dunes flanked by sweet-smelling pines, the odour of sea and sun and trees mingling together to form a fragrance both exciting and restful. The bird set him down there, in the centre of a grove that dappled the soil with light, yet shut out the hottest rays of the warm sun.

He lay on his back, watching the bird turn blackly against the sky and disappear beyond the ring of trees. He became aware of his size again, in the same way that a man becomes aware of his reality after awaking from a dream.

He stood up, suddenly conscious that he was fully accoutred in armour and weapons, even to his shield, which no longer bore the scratchings of the beast. He looked around and saw a path leading off through the pines towards a grassy slope that wound amongst the trees in neat-flanked order; enticing.

He followed it, seeking to control his feelings.

The path, as he had suspected it would, wound through the trees to a ridge overlooking the beach. From there, only the faintest hint of mist hung like sea-wrack over the ocean. Inland, the ground sloped down gently to a wide meadow that was flanked by colourful trees and dotted with clumps of coarse plants set out in such manner that a wanderer's feet were persuaded to the path.

He slung his shield upon his back and followed the path down through the meadow.

The grass was springy and fresh, sweet-smelling. Birds, tiny and bright-coloured, darted among the bushes along with butterflies. There was a constant susurration of wings and song, magnified by the soft, sweet breeze that came over the ridge, adding its own faint scent of pine to the lushness of the grass.

Beyond the meadow there rose a thick forest of gnarled trees, climbing up the flanks of a second ridge. They were darker and sturdier than the others, all sombre greens and earthy browns, interlaced with hints of red and yellow, as though seasons mingled together without reference to the time of natural changing. And at the edge of the forest there waited a white horse, decked out in golden fitments, with silver stirrups and silver bridle-metal. It stood quietly, a splash of brightness against the dark of the woods; waiting.

Spellbinder went to it. Mounted.

When he grasped the reins, the white horse turned and swung into a gallop faster than any natural steed could attain so quickly.

There was no need to grasp the reins other than to give hands some purchase against the speed of the horse's passing; not more need to direct it, for it knew where it was going. All that was left was to stay in the saddle and avoid the branches that threatened to sweep him clear of the saddle.

Up through the woodlands they went, and out on to a wide plain where the grass grew high as a man's head, cut through with tidy avenues that were flanked by neat little trees rich with fruit.

The horse galloped faster and faster, and as it did, the

fruits dropped from the trees and the grass withered, turning first to autumn's yellow, then to winter's black. The plain became white, covered with snow. The snow stirred up, shaken by a wind that came from nowhere, that pierced his body to the bone as it clustered white flakes about his face and burned his mouth with its chill. The horse continued to gallop, hoofs sprouting whirling white spray behind. The snow grew red, and a sound of roaring tumult howled over the waste. Ahead, there rose up a great mist of white-flecked red, like a snow storm coloured with blood, or a storm of blood flecked with bone.

The horse galloped headlong into the mist.

And sensation ended.

There was nothing. No feeling, no pain, no movement. Only the deep, blank *nothingness*.

He woke.

He opened his eyes, not truly aware of closing them, and saw a white room: white walls, white ceiling, white carpets covering the floor. A window: white glass illuminated by a white sun. He sat up, looking down at white sheets, white hands clutching them.

A door opened, and the room became coloured. White was replaced by the soft glow of amethyst, of crystal. The floor coverings assumed the hues of rich-woven carpets: red and green and blue and black and purple and gold mingling in patterns that dazzled his tired eyes. Tapestries hung on the walls, their shades complementing those of the carpets. Bright sun glazed through the window, the gold adding to the texture of the room. The glass of the window showed flaws that enhanced the light, sparking it off in patterns of yellow and silver and gold, illuminating the dust motes that danced in the air, accenting the blue of the sky beyond.

He looked up at the ceiling, and saw patterns of shadow floating lazily over a dome of blue-painted plaster, like peering into a pool of clear sea water.

He smiled and sank back against the luxuriously soft pillows, staring at the door.

A white-robed man stepped through, ducking his head a moment towards the bed, then stepping back to murmur something to the personage behind.

The door swung wider, and a tall man entered the room.

Regal of bearing he was, tall as Spellbinder himself, and as straight, as upright, though older. He was dressed in a white robe that hung down from broad shoulders in a single sweeping flow that did nothing to hinder his movements. His hair was black, silvered with strands of white. His eyes were the same colour: black flecked through with lightness. The dark tan of his skin threw them into stark relief against his fine-etched face, against the spread of wide cheek-bones cut by a proud nose above wide, full lips.

He stared at Spellbinder as a man might stare at some cherished painting, or a sculpture that was somehow flawed. There was love in his look, and anger; regret, too, and hope.

He came across the room and motioned for the other man to enter, taking two goblets from the tray the second carried.

Setting them down upon a slender-columned table whose surface was of a smooth marble flecked through with fine blue veins, he drew a plain chair up to the bed. The second man, shorter and younger than the patriarch, set down a flask of chased silver and paused a moment, as though awaiting instructions.

The older man said, "Thank you, Littol."

His voice was deep and measured, naturally commanding; the younger man inclined his head, withdrawing after glancing curiously at Spellbinder. The dark man watched the door close behind Littol, then turned to face the man in the seat. Curiosity existed in his gaze, too, though it was the interest of one who reviews a familiar object after some time of separation, assessing it, rekindling memories.

For a while silence filled the room. Then, as if he had decided the wordless examination had gone on long enough, the tall man lifted the silver decanter, filling both goblets. He passed one to Spellbinder.

"Welcome."

Spellbinder raised the goblet. "It has been a long time."

"Aye. Long enough. It pleases me to see you again,

though I would have had the manner of your coming somewhat different.''

"And I," grinned the dark man in the bed, "though I had little choice in the matter.''

He sipped the amber liquid contained in the goblet, savouring the taste, then glanced down at his body. As he had expected, his wounds were full healed, leaving no trace behind.

"You are mended," murmured the older man; absently, as if it were a foregone thing. "How came you to that raft?''

"You do not know?" Spellbinder was genuinely surprised. "I had assumed a pattern to exist.''

"Perhaps one does. I cannot see it, though; nor the Sighters. They would speak with you later, but for now, tell me of your coming.''

Briefly, in a conversation that was comprised of gestures and vocal inflections as much as of words, Spellbinder outlined the events leading up to his casting-away on Worldheart.

"How long I floated, I cannot say," he concluded. "Perhaps for three days, perhaps more. I was powerless until the bird came.''

"Aye. It was the bird warned us. We sent it questing. It found you.''

"And Raven?" queried Spellbinder. "What of her?''

The older man became grave. "We know not. There is no communion.''

Spellbinder lifted in the bed, his movement spilling wine in golden streamers over the coverings. He ignored the dampness, fixing the other's eyes with a glare of such intensity that the robed man blinked and set down his own goblet.

He raised a placatory hand, saying, "We have sought for her. That is one of the reasons you are to tell your story to the Assembly: that we may obtain a full picture, and thus strengthen our efforts.''

"She is gone, then? You have no vision?''

Spellbinder's voice was hoarse, anger and fear mingling.

"None as yet. Hopefully your contribution will enable us to form a contact of some kind.''

"By the Stone!" His tone was bitter now, resentful. "Mayhap she was right when she sought to let drop the burden."

"No." The older man shook his head, speaking gently. "Once the burden is taken up, there can be no putting down. You of all our people should know that."

"Aye, you speak truth." The bitterness remained. "I of all know that."

"Know, too, the weight is shared," said the robed one gently, rising from the chair. "Remember that." He turned towards the door. "I shall send food. Clothes are prepared for you, and the Assembly meets at sunset. Until then, compose your thoughts."

"I shall," nodded Spellbinder, his voice bleak. "Fear not, Talan. I shall."

The door closed, leaving him alone in the bright, light room with sunshine dancing over white and silver and gold; all bright. Only his thoughts were dark.

Six

"Look behind you: your friend may be sharpening his sword."

A tenet of the Corganii.

The hall was as he remembered it: high ceilings fluted with spanning arms of gold that offset the pure, alabaster white of the roof; walls of silver akin to the radiant shimmer of the northern glaciers, white and silver and blue mingling in a radiation of shades that effected a rainbow hue over the room; tall, smooth pillars of marbled white that reflected the multiple shades emanating from the walls and windows; the latter seemingly clear, but flecked through with colour—red, amber, black, blue, silver, gold, green—that added to the irradiation of the sun streaming in through the high orifices to light the tapestries and fitments so that the hall danced with light.

The doors that had closed behind him were of solid silver, so old that the carvings decorating the faces were grown black, adding a dimension of age and perspective to the original designs. The floor on which he trod was tiled in black marble, so dark that its sheening surface reflected the light and appeared almost silver.

At the far end of the great hall there stood a dais. By the standards of Karhsaam it was low: a slight platform of pure white against the darker floor, wide enough to accommodate three chairs of simple design and a small table. Around it were spaced twenty seats of carved gold, far grander than the chairs upon the dais. Each settle was occupied by a man or woman of indeterminate age, dressed in white robes.

The central space was occupied by three men. One was Talan; the others were older.

Spellbinder strode down the avenue formed by the pillars; halted facing the dais. He wore his armour: sword at

71

hip, shield on back. There was a murmur of surprise and shock.

"You bear arms here." The figure occupying the central chair of the dais was silver of hair, lined of face; age sat upon his features. "Why?"

"Do you ask why I carry them in the world?" answered Spellbinder. "Or have you forgotten what exists beyond the mist?"

"You presume too much." The man to the central figure's right spoke now. "You know the customs."

"Valar," said Spellbinder, "I know that you are ready to send others into a world you would not dabble in yourself. I know that Talan seeks knowledge for honest ends. I know that Quatar would find a melding of the patterns to benefit all men. I know that I was sent because my birthing damned me. Or saved me. If you would know what exists outside your island, listen. Watch, too. The world changes. It turns, Valar, and there is no way you—or any of us—may halt that turning. Better to understand than to change, for there is no longer any changing of it."

"That sits ill on your lips," said Valar. "The outcast? The changeling, telling us the policy of the turning?"

"My birth was not my doing," rejoined Spellbinder. "Lay not that blame on me, but upon those who spawned me. In love, Valar. An important thing in the outer world."

Talan's face grew pale beneath its natural darkness and he opened his mouth to speak, but Valar pre-empted him:

"A fortunate accident, for which we are all grateful. However, it does not resolve our problems."

"*No.*"

Quatar's voice was old and dry with the husking of ages and wisdom and understanding. It stilled both Valar and Spellbinder, and the whole murmur of conversation within the hall.

"*It does not.* And we are here to resolve those problems. For that we require total concentration, a joining of effort. Not a bickering. Spellbinder went into the world to act as our agent; he chose it, and has fared well. You, Valar, chose to stay here; and have worked doughtily for our aims. Now forget your arguments and concentrate on the matter in hand."

He lowered his grey head, staring at his hands as though to gather power, then turned to Spellbinder.

"Why do you wear armour here? The question seems relevant."

"I went into the world," answered Spellbinder, "as an emissary of your aims—the aims of the Assembly—I cannot shed those things it became needful to assume so easily as a tree might shed its leaves. I am not a thing of seasons, but of beliefs. I cannot forget a path so easily as a river might: if a dam is built against me I shall not run round it, but seek to tear it down and go through it."

"And you feel a similar obstacle is built against you now?" asked Quatar. "You no longer trust us?"

Talan spoke then, saying: "I told him we could not surmise the happenings, master. Not plan the pattern."

Quatar nodded as Valar shook his head in disbelief; or disapproval.

"There is no pattern," he said. "Only a trail of rough-woven events that lead to nowhere. Perhaps nowhere is where Spellbinder must go. Do you trust us?"

Spellbinder looked up at the old and ageless eyes. And bowed his head.

"Aye. You are the best the world has: I trust you."

"Then you will listen to me and take what I say as truth. And do it?"

"If it sits right with what I owe the world."

"With what you owe the woman called Raven?"

"That is it. I owe her a debt."

"Of love?"

"That and other things. We are companions—there is no breaking it."

"Then you must concede yourself to the Assembly. To find where she has gone."

"Not finally dead, then?" he asked. "I saw her taken down in fire by a creature that defied sword and arrow. That left me splintered; without magic. And you know not where she is?"

"No," said Quatar, "we do not know. But we shall find her."

"Will you promise me that?" asked Spellbinder. "That you will bend every effort of the Assembly to finding her?"

"She is important to us." An irritable note crept into Quatar's voice. "That was, of all the many choices, why she alone was chosen. We protect our own."

"I stretched on a Haral rack," said Spellbinder. "Devoid of power I sought words of my own devising to free us; myself and Raven. Where were you then?"

"Blind," said Quatar, simply. "Our sighting was cut off."

Spellbinder opened his mouth to speak again, but the silver-haired man cut him short.

"The evil that struck the last Summer Gathering was a bait," he said. "A *lure* set out to suck us in. We envisioned some hint of evil, but then lost it. Until this year's Gathering."

"So you knew of the evil, the thing the Vedast priests call the Black One," said Spellbinder. "Was that why we came to Haral?"

"In part," answered Quatar. "There was a need for investigation."

"And for death?" snarled the dark-clad warrior. "Was it needful that Raven should die?"

"She is not dead. Not necessarily. Her light is not yet dimmed in the pattern."

"I thought you had no pattern. I thought you could no longer see her." Spellbinder stared angrily at Talan.

"Patience was never a virtue of your birthing," the old man murmured. "Listen."

"For how long?" snarled the warrior-mage. "Until she is dead? Or is she dead now? And you lying to me?"

The insult stilled the Assembly as might a hard-given slap quell a nervous voice. Spellbinder spoke out over the stillness.

"I need answers. You chose me to go into the world, so now let me choose the manner of my going therein. You selected me to guide and govern Raven. Do you now expect me to forget her? Is that the measure of your trust?"

The answer that came to him was soundless, voiceless: a whispering in his mind that said *No . . . No, not that. Not ever that.*

"What then?" he cried, aloud. "Tell me."

*   *   *

"She is a worldshaper," said Quatar, "a changer. She may not like her role, but it is hers: irrevocable, unchangeable. Consequently this new occurrence must hinge on that premise—the manner in which she went suggests an alternative power. One of death and decay."

"Find her," said Spellbinder bluntly. "Team the Sighters to find her. Or must I go alone?"

"Ultimately, yes," said Quatar. "You and the bird. Perhaps some few others; beyond that I do not know."

"Then find it. Know it," Spellbinder snarled. "Or I go from here alone."

"Wait." The sage's voice was gentle. "Why think you the whole Assembly gathers here? To find your Raven, and the evil that took her."

"Find it," grunted Spellbinder. "Then send me after it. I ask no more."

There was no visible movement, only a mental shifting, a closing in of minds. It was as though barriers closed about him or tentacled sea-beasts, their protuberances suckering into his brain. For a while there was blackness; after, a sense of draining, of emptiness. He was aware of knowledge passing outwards, vaguely aware of incoming strengths.

"Now you have it," he said when the weakening was passed, "all of it."

"Not all," said Quatar, "but enough to sense a pattern. It will take time to assess. Time to devolve a plan."

"And Raven?" asked the dark man. "Must she wait, too?"

"For the moment, yes. Until we can assess this thing there is nothing we can do to help her. I must allow that we seem helpless at the time, and cannot aid her. You, Spellbinder, must wait. Word will come."

"Is she dead?" he shouted. "Tell me!"

"Death is but a word," said Quatar. "In a word: yes, she is dead, for we are unable to find her, and so she must be gone into those regions where life does not exist."

"Then send me after her," Spellbinder snarled. "I'll forfeit life to bring her back."

"Perhaps you shall," said the old man gently. "You may have promised more than you think."

Seven

"Action that is not directed by knowledge is usually wasted, thus the truly strong man must learn the virtue of patience."

The Books of Kharwhan.

Time is merely a word. The sun rises, travels across the sky, and sets, bringing darkness: the cycle repeats itself. Should a man be hooded, set afloat in water of the same temperature as his body, and that sheathed in some garment as will deny him the sense of touch, then time becomes meaningless. He knows that time passes, but an instant in darkness lasts far longer than an instant of the same duration in light. The assassin, crouched with knife in hand, holding his breath in a dark room as he awaits the turning of a key in the door, experiences more time than the innocent victim who is merely performing a routine motion: time is subjective.

So it was for Spellbinder as he waited on the Sighters of Kharwhan.

His attitude whilst attending the Assembly had disturbed many of the leaders of that secret community, adding to the difficulty inherent in the sorting of an already confused situation. Thus his own impatience delayed him: he was forced to wait until such time as a clear pattern be unravelled from the tangled skeins of fate.

The days passed slowly, each moment seeming—feeling—to take him farther from Raven.

In a way, he was surprised. The nature of their companionship was free: they had been parted before, and he knew that the woman enjoyed lovers other than himself, which had never worried him. Death had been their companion for too long to allow him the luxury of pretending such finality did not exist: he had thought himself at terms with that ultimate truth.

Yet now he chafed at every delaying moment, pestering

for information that was not available until the painstaking sifting of fact and possibility, the balancing of reality with surmise, was completed.

He wandered the streets of Kharwhan's only city, taking some small enjoyment from those reminders of his past, wondering even now at the magnificence of the place.

The city had no name, for with no other on the island it seemed pointless to assign nomenclature. It spread over several thousand klis, standing out from a vast meadow of verdant grass, in which played animals and birds and butterflies. Beyond the meadow there were trees. Lush orchards to the south and east, the sweet scent of their fruit brought to the city by the gentle breeze from the sea, the gay colours decking the green branches with myriad hues. To the west and north the timber grew darker, wilder, the verdancy of the orchards giving way to gnarled oaks and tall pines, slender elms, regal birches, and other species no longer nameable. These latter forests spread out in glorious profusion, hiding secret meadows and little brooks where clean, cool water chanted plainsong over stones that hid darting fish and croaking frogs. Dragonflies darted buzzing wings over the water, and the iridescent flash of knightfishers and parrots danced colour through the dappled shading of the trees.

Towards the northern extremity of the Ghost Isle there rose up a mountain that was capped with snow. It was visible from the balconies of the city, its lower slopes thick with timber, interspersed with meadows of lush grass. A waterfall cascaded down one flank, the silver spray hued with rainbow colours in the sun. Dark, granite and black obsidian melded together beneath the purest white of snow; there were veins of sandstone shining yellow; and washes of clay, red as blood from a distance.

Like all of Kharwhan's surface, the mountain was a creation of willpower, a melded thing that contained the finest aspects of beauty and creation, without the ugliness of reality.

The city was the same.

To approach it was to see a mountain of white, all spires and fluted walkways. Closer up, the individual hues became apparent: where vaulted towers thrust clean, lean, white lines against the azure of the sky, there were veins of blue and gold and red. Patches of rusty ochre stood out; black; green, in all its many shades, from the soft stridency of unripe apples to the deepness of autumn's leaves. The spires and towers hung rather than stood, as if the sky itself dangled them, their windows glinting gold and silver in the light. Between them, like webs strung across the heavens, there were balconies and walkways, their sides cut through with intricate patterns so that they appeared nebulous; fragile. The streets were paved with blocks of gold and platinum and marble; with obsidian and chalcedony and amethyst. And between the blocks were gaily flowering plants, shrubs, bushes. Directions were marked by flora rather than signs, a hedge of purple sage directing the way around a corner where a low hall of silver-streaked marble gave way to a tower of blue slate; a spread of crimson roses leading on to a spire that was ivory at its base, then roseate coral, the succulent green of seaweed or aged metal, all covered with verdigris; and then the red of honest brick, interlaced with grey clay and silver threads. Above that might hang a balcony of crystal, transparent, fragile. Above, a slender peak of silver or obsidian or gold.

To look upon the city was to produce the same effect as when you rub knuckles against tired eyes and produce a kaleidoscope of colour: it was every colour in multiple assembly, dazzling; almost frightening. It was ethereal; unreal.

Spellbinder wondered at it, comparing it with the cities of the outside world. It was incompatible; separate in time and formation and belief.

He borrowed a horse from Talan and rode into the forests, exploring the forgotten trails that wound through the groves towards the mountain or the beaches.

He spent one day staring at the sea, watching the waves pound on rocks thick with barnacles and mussels, thinking that he stared towards Kragg, where Gondar Lifebane ruled.

Another day he lay on silver sand, soft to the touch, unclinging and warm, watching an ocean that was gentle, its waves lapping like soft tongues against the beach. And looked southwards to where Argor the mercenary held his keep.

And then he was summoned: the Assembly had obtained a pattern from the Sighters.

There were only four men in the room: Spellbinder, Quatar, Talan and Valar.

The room was small, a simple place built quietly within the confines of the main Assembly hall. It was windowed on only one side, that opening set with plain glass that allowed the final rays of the sun to illuminate the men seated within. They sat in plain chairs, and already there were lanterns lit against the mounting dark. They sat around a plain table of simple wood, devoid of ornament or decoration. They were sombre.

Spellbinder fought to contain his impatience, running his fists over his knees as he waited for Quatar to speak.

At last, voice dry, the old man announced the findings of the Sighters.

"We do not know," he said. "Not for sure. There is a strangeness abroad, like a shadow on the world."

"And Raven?" demanded Spellbinder. "What of her?"

Quatar shrugged. "Alive, as best we can tell."

"Where?" the dark man demanded. "May I reach her?"

"Not yet. Listen, that your impatience does not hinder your judgement. Stay still a while, that you may acquaint yourself with all the facts. Will you receive us?"

"Aye," nodded Spellbinder. "But know that I shall seek her, whatever."

"We know that," said Quatar. "We knew that from the start or we'd not have chosen you. Now be still and hear us."

Spellbinder nodded again and settled into a position of repose. Quatar bowed his head, and beside him Talan and Valar did the same.

The voices were soundless, entering his mind as thoughts and impressions rather than vocalisations. He answered in the same fashion, reducing their dialogue to a minimum.

A power has entered the world from beyond the mountains, the ones called World's End.

The Shadow Lords?

No. This is older. Worse. It knows Kharwhan and has force enough to blind our seeing. It was able to set a blanket on its doings of sufficient strength that you became powerless.

Why did it take Raven?

It needs her.

How do you know? I thought your sighting was dimmed.

Fact on estimate. It set a bait: you came. It might have taken you: it did not; took Raven: wanted (needed) her alone.

Have you sought other advice?

Our emissaries have gone out to Quell, to the Valley of Uthaan, and all the other oracles. They report the self-same message: ruin and death.

So what must I do?

Find her. Bring her back. Worldchanger, she, not to be lost. If this other power can find a way to use her, then it might focus such forces through her that we can no longer stem them.

Would that be a bad thing?

You have been a long time in the world outside. Do you really think that men can run their own affairs? Do they not need guidance?

Help, mayhap; advice. But guidance? Control? Should they not be left to govern their own doings? And suffer whatever consequences stem therefrom?

Would you leave a child to play with swords?

Yes. Warning it that the blade might cut.

And when it does?

Then I shall tell it of the powers of a blade, and explain why such things are not toys.

But the baby would still bleed.

Yes, it would. For a while. But then the wound would be bandaged; afterwards the child would know how a sword can cut. Know, too, that such a thing is not a toy.

Nor is destiny.

No, but you set destiny on Raven as might a careless parent hand a blade to a child. To wield it as you designed; that sets a responsibility on you.

We seek to fashion a world. To make it better.

Your beliefs are admirable, but for whom? Can you shape a world?

We do that. Now.

From here, from Kharwhan. From an island shrouded in mist. Where trees grow at your bidding, and snow always decks the mountain. Where your orchards flesh fruit at your calling, and the beaches run foam in accordance with your desires.

What else would you have us do?

Go out into the world. Forget Kharwhan and its mists. Learn how people live.

And leave the running of it to the ordinary people?

Why not? They live there, in that world you govern without entering. Does their presence not entitle them to some say in their own lives?

Would that help them? Would they be the better for it?

Perhaps not. Physically, at least. Spiritually, it might be to their advantage.

So you, who know them so well, would make this decision?

Perhaps.

Would they be better for it? Better without Kharwhan's governance?

Perhaps.

Would you make the decision?

Perhaps.

Make it, then. Say Yea or Nay on our interference.

And Raven? What of her?

She is alone. Like all the others.

You hang me in quandary. How can I choose?

Quatar's mind chuckled. *You see our problem. It is needful that someone chooses. Forces such as this power in Xandrone must be fought. The mortals lack the necessary abilities, so the burden falls to us.* He fell silent a moment, raising his ancient, tired face to stare at Spellbinder. The waning sun illumined his silver hair, etching shadows on his features: he smiled.

We are not gods, my son, merely different. We of Kharwhan are gifted with certain abilities in the same manner as some men are gifted with swordskill, or a talent for paint. It is our duty to utilise those talents as best we may. Some claim this ability a curse, but the burden, once lifted, may not be easily released.

You digress, Quatar. Valar's mindvoice was cool, impatient. *Tell him what he must do and be done with it.*

Spellbinder glanced at the man, making no attempt to shield the irritation flooding his mind.

You were ever impatient, Valar. That fault may someday prove your downfall.

At your hand? There was contemptuous laughter. *You lack the strength.*

Spellbinder smiled, though no humour showed in his eyes. He touched the hilt of his sword, speaking aloud. In the stillness of the room the words rang loud, menacing.

''Your strength is mental. The keenest brain may still be silenced with a blade.''

Too long in the world! His tainted blood affects the crudities of men.

Valar! Be silent!

For one so old, Quatar was yet able to send a whiplash of mental energy through the room. Valar shut his mind, hurt.

This bickering serves no purpose other than to delay our action. Talan ''spoke'' for the first time, seeking to placate, to find a balance. *Let these differences be forgotten. Let us discuss the matter in hand.*

Sense, Quatar agreed. *Our immediate problem supercedes these personal differences.*

Spellbinder emanated reluctant agreement.

As best our sighting can tell it, came the thought, *this evil stems from some point far to the west of Xandrone. It has found an entry point through which it can feed. It seeks to spread its power, knowing that we shall oppose it. For that end, it has taken Raven, knowing her to be a focus. Our prognostications suggest that it will use her to unite such a force as might spread Xandronian rule across the world, and ultimately conquer this island. It must be halted, its cancer stopped.*

How shall I do it? Spellbinder accepted the duty without question. *Where do I find her?*

You must go west. Your own senses will tell you where she is. That, or the force will recognise the threat you represent.

Alone?

Do you require help?

Xandrone is wide and savage. It is as well to watch one's back.

Who would you take with you?

Without hesitation he thought, *Argor and Gondar Lifebane.*

Granted. Come next sun's set, they shall await you where the Horn River passes Xin.

In the tavern known as the Goat, added Valar. *A fitting name.*

Spellbinder ignored the comment.

"Very well." He rose, using his voice now that the mental communication was ended. "I shall be ready."

Quatar nodded, seeming satisfied with the outcome. Talan, though, appeared concerned, while Valar ignored Spellbinder, fixing his gaze upon the table until the dark man was gone from the room.

Spellbinder felt the hostility, but ignored it, assuming Valar's dislike to stem from the basic differences inherent in their personalities and their birthing. There were, in any event, other matters occupying his thoughts. He paced the streets, pondering the difficulty of his mission, sifting those facts vouchsafed him by Quatar and the others, seeking to establish his own pattern.

Raven was not dead. Nor was she in the world of the living. Therefore whatever had taken her must hold her in limbo. Where in the wastes of Xandrone that limbo, or some entry thereto, might be was up to him to discover. Equally was it up to him to unravel the mystery of the kidnap, the nature of this unknown force. And halt it.

He paused, suddenly realising that he had wandered into a section of the city with which he was not familiar. The buildings were somewhat smaller here, of more recent appearance than the magnificent conglomeration filling the centre. He looked about him, feeling strangely out of place. These houses, for all their fanciful designs, were simple homes: the smell of cooking wafted on the cool night air, and from open windows came the laughter of children, the warm glow of lights, the murmur of conversation. Spellbinder experienced the unfamiliar sensation of loneliness. Once he had known the city in all its details, the streets and parks had been his playground, he had clambered amongst the walkways and balconies, visited friends. Now the place was grown larger, spreading out, and he was a stranger; a visitor, rather than a citizen.

Momentarily, depression washed over him: he no longer belonged in Kharwhan, yet neither was he truly of the outside world. He smiled cynically, beginning to retrace his steps: he was outlaw, outlander, wherever he might travel. But so, he mused, was Raven; so, too, Argor; in a way, Gondar. The thought cheered him with its reminder of the free companionship of the sword, of the road. It would be good to stand again shoulder to shoulder with such fellows.

An invitation from Talan awaited him on his return to has chambers. He bathed and donned a robe of black silk: his gesture had been made, and there was no longer need to emphasise his difference with blade and armour. Besides, Talan was a friend.

His living quarters occupied several floors of a tower joined to Spellbinder's rooms by an arching bridge. The walkway was an ephemeral creation of filigree metalwork, a web-like construction that appeared to be fashioned from platinum and gold and black Quwhon steel. Its floor was an intricate mesh of metals set within clear crystal, so that its crossing was as though one walked on air. The tower beyond was comprised of black stone at its base, overlaid with sheets of beaten copper and etched bronze. Around the level of the first storey ran a series of windows, taller than a tall man and set so close together that the higher levels seemed to rest on a blanket of silvery light. Red brick and amethyst, topaz and obsidian and garnet formed the next two levels, all worked together as though melted and poured out through a funnel. There was marble in all its many hues, and metals—silver, steel, gold, platinum— worked together to create a fantastic concoction of styles and colours and textures that blended against all odds to form a weirdly beautiful creation.

The room into which Spellbinder was ushered was simple in comparison. Dark wood formed the floor, the lanterns set along the circular walls throwing up the deep colouration. A table of the same wood occupied the centre, set round with four chairs of carved marble. Plain drapes of plum-coloured velvet were drawn over the windows, their texture lending a sense of seclusion and secrecy to the room. The walls were of smooth, bluish-grey granite, devoid of ornamentation other than the silver fitments of the lanterns and a straight-bladed sword fastened with wooden pegs over the empty fireplace.

The sword was long and clean and sharp. Its guard was a curved arc of silver, traced through with threads of gold. The hilt was leather; black by nature, but stained deeper with hand's sweat, the markings of usage outlining where the fingers had rested. The pommel was of the same design as the guard, a clawed cup holding a massive emerald, the jewel's facets cut so that the gem ended in a point under which flesh might be scored.

Talan sat lonely beneath the blade. He toyed with a goblet of wine, and rose anxiously as Spellbinder entered the room.

He saw the younger man's gaze fasten on the sword, and filled a second goblet, gesturing for Spellbinder to seat himself.

"Tara and the children dine elsewhere," he said. "I thought it best we speak alone."

"The sword is still in place." Spellbinder sat down, accepting the wine. "I thought you had forgotten it."

"Your father's blade? No! He strove too hard to form a balance. To equate this island of ours to the outside world. He saw farther than any of us: hence your duties."

"Duties?" Spellbinder sipped his wine. "Would Valar agree they are duties?"

"Valar is ambitious," said Talan, "he believes we are élite. And so removed."

"And you?"

"Need you ask?"

"Forgive me. No: I do not. But I am troubled."

"So was your father. He saw the danger of our powers, and chose to temper them with that thing called humanity."

"Aye," Spellbinder nodded. "I was the result of that experiment. Has it worked, uncle?"

"I believe so," said Talan. "You appear formed in reasonable shape and intelligence. Your mind is sane, and your work fulfills your father's aims."

"Would Valar agree?"

"Valar is ambitious and proud, but he has only one voice."

"Loud, though."

"Aye, but not so loud it can overcome Quatar, or myself."

"I have powerful allies."

"Are you bitter? Should I have claimed nepotism to your support?"

"No. That would have defeated the purpose: I shall do what I must. Tomorrow I shall go to Xandrone and find Raven. If it is feasible, then I shall destroy this force. Whatever it might be."

"All help I can grant you, I shall." Talan ran slender fingers about the rim of the goblet. "But I fear there is little. This power is strong: you might well fall to it."

"No man lives for ever," said Spellbinder, emphasising the *man*.

"Valar may seek to block you." Talan was embarrassed; the words came only with difficulty. "He does not approve. Be careful, there. What help I can give, I shall."

"I know," said Spellbinder. "I know, also, that you are a good, true friend. If you can guard my rear, from Kharwhan, and I have Gondar and Argor with me on the other side, then we may fight clear."

Talan nodded. "It will be hard."

"Has it not ever been? Was it easy to find Raven? To find the shaper of worlds? The crux point?"

"No," said Talan. "That finding was mightily hard."

"But she was found. I was sent to her. I brought her to you, so now I must find her again."

"For our reasons, or your own?" said Talan. "We must state them honestly between us."

"Both." Spellbinder's tone was flat. "I love her, there is no denying it: I will chance all to find her."

"All of Kharwhan?" asked Talan. "Would you bring down this island for her?"

"If I must. I want her back. I will not let her lay with

some demon god. I shall bring her back even though it means all Kharwhan comes down in ruin.''

"So you would destroy it all?"

"Yes: I would: I want her back."

"You chance much," said Talan. "A great risk."

"Perhaps. But given the choice of happiness and duty, which would you choose? Who argues better: friends who have proved themselves, or the state that governs their business?"

"The state knows more," said Talan. "It must."

"But friends give more," said Spellbinder. "Which is more important?"

"You pose a conundrum, a riddle."

"No. Does my duty rest with Raven or Kharwhan?"

"With both, surely; they are linked."

"But if they differ? Then what? Confusion: I must choose between them."

"What would you choose?"

"Raven," said Spellbinder. "Always."

Eight

"A man needs three things in which he can trust:
himself, his sword, and his friends."

A proverb of Kragg.

Xin sprawled along the southern bank of the Horn River,
where the waterway described a sweeping curve through
the flatlands. On the north side the ground was too swampy
for building, too populous with stinging insects and poisonous reptiles. On the south side, it was merely uncomfortable.

Wharves and jetties stuck out into the river where the
widest angle of the great ox-bow afforded the most room
for trading craft to find a berth, behind them a scattering of
warehouses and stockyards. Farther inland, where the ground
rose slightly, were the buildings of the city itself. Timber
they were, in the main part, though a few edifices of stone
existed; all built up on piles to raise them a Xand's height
above the moist soil, and none taller than two levels.
Mostly they were long, squat buildings, surrounded by
verandahs with ornately carved stairs going down to the
rough-paved streets. Windows and doors were spaced along
the balconies, the names or emblems of the occupants
carved into the hard timber. Beneath the houses Xands
were penned, though the largest concentrations of the animals were in the yards beside the river or the corrals lying
southwest of the city.

Smoke drifted in lazy spirals from the chimneys, and
here and there early lamps were lit against the encroaching
night. Birds sang as they hurried nestwards, and over the
river a handful of gulls culled the last pickings of the day
from the somnolent water.

Amongst the river craft berthed for the night one vessel
stood out. Lean and low, her flanks black-painted, the
single mast boasting a furled sail of the same night's black

as her boards, the wolf-boat shifted lazily in the stream, like some great predator taking her rest. The prow was carved in the fashion of a snarling wolf, a red-painted tongue curling between white fangs, crimson eyes inset with polished roundels of jet. Four men crouched at the stern, where the blue eyes depicting the All-Mother were carved and painted on the huge steering oar. A keg of bitter sea ale stood close by; the men rolled dice and grumbled.

"How long do we squat here like old women?" demanded one. "We might have sacked this place ere now and be sailing homeward."

"Ask Gondar, Torfi," answered the man closest to the ale keg.

"If you dare," added another.

"By the Mother!" grunted the one called Torfi. "I'll do that if we sit like beggars at a feast much longer."

"And beg for something else," came the reply.

"For what? Torfi Swiftsword begs for nothing."

"What has two arms, two legs, but cannot see or hear, though it moves?"

"You play me riddles, Gathlac? While we squat and turn our thumbs to women's games?"

"Answer the riddle and see the sense, Torfi."

"I cannot."

"Then I shall tell you the answer," grinned Gathlac. "A man has two arms and two legs, but he cannot see or hear without his head. But if Gondar Lifebane lopped it from his shoulders he would still move. For a little while."

Torfi grunted and helped himself to ale. "So we must wait while the Lifebane concludes whatever mysterious business we sailed so far to find?"

"Aye," said Gathlac. "We must wait. Gondar Lifebane is Lord of Kragg, our liege-lord. If Gondar deemed it needful we come to this swampy midden of a place and wait here, then wait we must. That is our duty, and he will have his reasons."

"There are times," grumbled Torfi, "that his reasons are so shrouded in mystery they seem like a rocky coast hidden behind mist."

But the thought of incurring the Lifebane's wrath stilled his questioning, and after a while the dice began to click on the scrubbed planks again.

On the farther perimeter of Xin, where the hardwood fences penned the Xands, a similar conversation took place.

Three men, dressed in a mixture of armour and leather, hunkered about a cook fire close beside a small corral in which nine horses munched on grass. A flask of Saran wine passed amongst the men, and they cast frequent glances about them, as though constantly expecting an attack. Where the reivers from Kragg had kept axes and bows close at hand, these three wore swords and throwing stars, and their faces were tanned by sun rather than sea wind, their muscles trimmed by riding rather than boat-faring.

"Blood of the Stone!" one muttered. "How long do we wait?"

"Until Argor bids us leave, Gerntius. Not before."

"Pah! You were ever the old man's lackey, Thius."

Hands fell to sword hilts, and the third man spoke quickly to damp the growing embers of anger.

"There was a reason for our coming, Gerntius. What it was, only Argor knows, but there was a reason."

"That he keeps to himself, Hyran! We fared well in the south. Would have fared better, had that bird not come. Stone's piss! We quit a fine trade route to ride here, to this piss-pile of miserable huts."

"You are new-come to the band," said Thius. "You do not know the affinity of Argor and the bird."

"I know the stories," grunted Gerntius irritably. "How the bird is linked to the one called Raven. How Argor trained the woman. But where is she? Argor sits in comfort with the sea-reiver while we crouch in the night, blowing on our hands to keep warm."

"We've known colder nights," said Hyran. "And wineless."

"But always with a purpose!" Gerntius accepted the flask, taking a long draught. "Now we wait with wine, but devoid of knowledge."

"Argor wishes it," said Thius. "Is that not enough?"

"Not for me," said Gerntius. "I need more reason."

"Then go and ask him," said Hyran. "We'll stand your watch. And when he's killed you, Argor will send someone to take your place."

Gerntius snarled and looked away to where the horses browsed calmly on the sweet river grass.

"I'll stay," he said reluctantly. "I'd not cross blades with Argor."

The tavern of the Goat occupied all of one building in Xin. Beneath the place were stalls for the guests' animals, the upper level was divided into rooms where visitors might find rest or whatever other comfort they required; the first level was given over to the drinking hall. It was a long, wide, low-ceilinged room, divided by twin rows of pillars and three great fireplaces. At intervals along the walls there were alcoves from which serving women brought drinks, and at one end stood a kitchen and wide tables.

On this particular night, as on the three preceding, ever since the wolf-boat had oared in to the jetty and the hardfaced riders had come from the south, the hall was further divided by human groupings.

One side of the room was occupied by inhabitants of Xandrone; citizens of Xin, traders, herders, freelance riders sat talking in their own language. On the other side, speaking together, but still clustered in their own groups, sat the men from the wolf-boat and the southern riders. Alone, facing one another over a broad table that was stained with wine and food, there were two men; giants, some might have called them.

One was a huge man, a head at least over any other present, his shoulders knotted with muscle, his hands dwarfing the goblet he held. A great thick mane of blond hair tumbled over his neck, bound back by a fillet of gem-mounted gold. His eyes were the grey of a storm-kissed sea bound in by the crags of his face, his beard was the same colour as his hair and as luxuriant as that wild growth covering his head. He wore a simple tunic of dark sea-stained leather, set about with silver plates, that exposed arms akin to the limbs of a half-grown oak. A wide belt spanned his waist; sheathed thereon, a double-headed throwing-axe, a short sword and a dirk. His legs were clad in tight, salt-whitened breeches tucked into knee-high boots of leather and metal.

He was somewhat drunk. He was Gondar Lifebane, Lord of Kragg, leader of the sea-reivers.

The man facing him was shorter by perhaps a head, but muscled as heavily. Older, his leonine tangle streaked through with grey, his beard a mingling of red fire and grey smoke. His chest was bare save for a metal-link vest in which hung throwing stars. At his waist he carried a long, straight-bladed sword of Tirwand steel and a curved dagger. A leather kirtle, reinforced with black steel discs, covered his loins, below which his legs were bare and brown and hairy until they disappeared into high boots of soft Yr leather.

This was Argor the mercenary; outlaw; leader of the southern horsemen.

He was at that same pleasant stage of drunkenness as Gondar: where senses remain alert, but life seems good and all men your friend. Until they prove otherwise.

"Where is he?" Gondar demanded. "Mother's Dugs! I gave up a fat merchantman to come here. Three days and as many nights we waited off the Dark Islands for sight of that Saran ship. It carried Xands and grass that I might have ransomed had the bird not called me."

"I suffered the same loss," Argor consoled. "Word had it that a slave train was bound north for the Altanate. Joined with a trader's caravan, too. I gave up all when the word came."

"Aye." Gondar shrugged, tilting the wine flask. "But what matters profit when Raven calls?"

Argor nodded and called for a fresh flask.

"Today at sun's set," he reminded. "That was when the bird said Spellbinder would come. That Raven needed us."

"And I'd storm the gates of every godly palace to find her," avowed Gondar. "I'd fight gods in her name."

"Mayhap you shall," said Argor. "For I cannot imagine why we both should be summoned so forcibly with pleas in her name unless there was some mighty danger."

The serving girl brought their new flask. She set it down

carefully, trying hard to stay out of reach of their hands, for her thighs were already bruised by their touching and she was frightened of these huge men and their ways.

Behind her, a door opened, letting in a brief wafting of sour marsh air and a man in a black cloak who glanced round and then strode directly towards the two captains.

They looked up as the man halted beside their table.

Gondar Lifebane laughed and said, "Stranger, we have no time for pedlars. What we want, we take."

More gently, Argor said, "Go away, stranger. We are disussing important things and do not have time for those we do not know."

"You have time for this," said Spellbinder, throwing back the hood of his cloak. "For that is why you came here."

"I do not understand. You say this creature took Raven while you were powerless? I saw you defeat Belthis in magical battle when I thought that wizard the mightiest alive."

Spellbinder nodded at Gondar, and said, "Yes. But this force is new. Belthis relied on the old powers. Whatever has Raven now is something unknown."

"And your alliance," Argor chose his words with far more tact than might be expected of a mercenary outlaw, "with the bird and the island cannot show where she is?"

"No." Spellbinder shook his head. "She is gone. All I know is that whatever took her came from the west. That she no longer exists on the plane of life, but is not necessarily dead. And that I must find her."

He paused, accepting the glass Gondar offered.

"It may well be a pointless task, but when asked what help I required, I said: Gondar and Argor. Will you come with me?"

Gondar reached down to lift his axe from the sheath. The twin-headed blade lifted as swiftly as a rising lark. And fell as fast as a stooping falcon. The glasses jumped, overturning as the blade bit the wood of the table. Wine ran like blood from the edges.

"Should I fail you," said the Lifebane, "you must take that axe and sever my right hand from the arm. Then use the thing to stuff my mouth as you cleave off my head.''

Argor nodded and said, ''Gondar speaks truth. We are akin. Him and me. You and me. If I fail you, use the same blade.''

Gondar said: ''I have a wolf-boat on the river. We can sail upstream to Lake Xand or the mountains. Thirty axes will back you.''

Argor said: ''I have only nine men, but they have horses. They can ride. They will die for me. Or Raven.''

Spellbinder, sad, said: ''No. It is not that kind of battle. We must go alone. We three. I sense it that way. Send them back.''

''Where do we travel?'' asked Gondar. ''I do not argue, but my men will need answering.''

''To meet death,'' said Spellbinder. ''But tell them to stand out beyond the Dark Islands for one night after their journey down the river and they will meet a merchantman bound for Lyand. The pickings will satisfy them.''

''And my riders?'' demanded Argor. ''What of them?''

''Go south from Xin towards the valley of Uthaan,'' said Spellbinder. ''Continue south and east in the direction of the coast. They will find a packtrain of slaves and wine and metal. It will keep them happy.''

''So we go alone,'' said Argor. ''So be it.''

In the morning both crews were sent off. They liked it little, but were given less choice. The promises made by Spellbinder went some way to dampening their objections, and at least set them to going with the bait of plunder in their minds.

The three captains departed in the opposite direction, mounted on horses, for Gondar proved incapable of riding a Xand and both Spellbinder and Argor preferred a stallion to the massive, uncomfortable spine of the horned beast of Xandrone.

''Where are we going?'' asked the suddenly land-straddled sea-reiver. ''Is it far?''

''Far enough,'' replied Spellbinder as Argor laughed. ''There is an oracle between here and Srygar that may tell us something. Besides, it is on our way.''

"Way where?" asked Gondar. "You said this force is in the west. My boat could have taken us there."

Spellbinder shook his head. "No, friend Gondar. Your boat could never have taken us."

"Why not?" demanded the reiver-king. "Where water is, I go."

"There is a difference now," said Spellbinder. "So it goes."

Nine

"Darkness hides many shadows. The blind man cannot
see them, though to the sighted they are clear as day."
The Books of Kharwhan.

Pain. That was the first thing she felt.

Then darkness, if the absence of light may be *felt,* even
though it seemed that she did.

Then a strange, curious absence of knowledge; as if, in
dreaming, she was simultaneously aware and unaware.
Conscious of happenings; yet unconscious of reality.

The pain ended and she was in darkness. It was a warm
darkness, almost friendly. It wrapped about her like a
warm blanket; as might the blanket of a child camouflage
the infant from nightmares that lurk outside the confines,
waiting to tear in should the blanket be lifted for an instant
to let in the rending horrors of dream.

For a while she stayed there, enjoying it.

Then she remembered that she was Raven: her own
woman: she opened her eyes.

She was in a room without windows. A black room, the
walls devoid of colour. The sheets covering her bed were
black. The floor was black: all was black.

She ran hands down her body and found herself nude.

She groped around the bed in search of weapons: found
none.

She rose and paced out the terminations of the floor
from wall to wall and back again to the bed.

There was nothing: no hint of door or window, no sign
of armour or blade.

Nothing . . .

Light entered the room. Blind . . . blazing . . . dimming her sight so that she shrunk in upon herself, dazzled,
one arm lifted to guard her blinded eyes, the other protective of her body, ready to strike.

97

"Why do you fear me? Have I hurt you?"

She began to protest, then realised that all her hurts were mended: there was no longer pain, or scar; nothing.

"You see? There is no pain where I command."

"Who are you? What are you?" Raven huddled on the bed: the only sure point in that universe of black and brilliance. "Why have you brought me here?"

"Because you pivot worlds." The voice from out the dazzle was soft and gently soothing. "Because you are unhappy with Kharwhan. Why should the sorceror-priests govern this world? Why should they dictate your actions? Why should you not be free?"

It was, in a way, like listening to a dream: the voice was hypnotic in its softness, as reassuring as the child's blanket; persuasive.

"Why do you hide? asked Raven. "Why not come openly?"

The light dimmed, faded down to a soft golden glow that outlined a god-like figure. Simultaneously, the room became lit, so that the figure in the door was both emphasised from behind and illuminated from in front.

The light played over golden hair framing a face that was both gentle and masculine, containing sufficient softness in its contours to be reassuring, and enough hard, craggy planes that it was equally demanding. The hair was pale as Raven's own, maned back in tumbled waves that touched the shoulders. They were wide and corded with muscle, as was the chest, set above a flat, bronzed stomach. A kirtle of plain white spanned the hips, covering the manhood of the creature, but exposing muscular legs adorned with golden hair. His arms were corded like a sea-reiver's, though the hands were long-fingered. Gentle as they held a tray on which rested a golden decanter and two silver goblets.

"Drink," he said, coming into the room. "We'll take wine together and speak of Kharwhan."

"Why?" asked Raven. "What knowledge do you seek of the Ghost Isle?"

"Everything. All you can tell me." His voice was soft and deep. "I heard you cry out against its strictures, seeking freedom. I offer you that."

He set the tray down on a table she had not noticed before, and filled two goblets with liquid. The goblets were chased silver, wound round with figures of men and women and animals.

Raven sipped the wine: it was soft and dry; refreshing.

The man sat down on the edge of the bed, smiling at her.

"All that opposes Kharwhan need not be evil," he said, prefacing her thoughts. "Do you not feel the Ghost Isle dictates too much? Surely, if the sorcerer-kings wanted only to help mankind, then they would make themselves clear; advise. Why do they hide?"

Raven looked at him, admiring his figure, enticed by his voice and eyes.

She looked again at the eyes. And saw that they had no pupils: were, merely, pools of blue without centre or focus other than the hypnotic stare emanating like the sun's gaze from the blank centres.

"You lie!"

Abruptly, as she said it, the wine turned to bitter acid in her mouth.

She spat it out, gagging on the sour taste of urine. And when she raised her head the golden man was turned to black, all black like a burned thing with red eyes staring out from crisped skin out of which lapped a snake-like tongue.

The room went dark again, illuminated only by the eyes and mouth of the . . . thing that had been a man.

"Of course I lie. I am the god of lies. I can turn your life to a lie. I can lay with you if I choose, but you are yet too petty a little human. You must learn my ways before I favour you."

There was a darkness deeper than before. Not night, not shuttered windows, nor closing doors, but absence of life. Raven whimpered in fear, her body chilled by the anger of the creature.

"And you will learn!" The voice echoed like thunder about the invisible confines of the blank room. "I swear you will learn!"

Raven clutched her arms about her body to still her terror and her trembling, and called out in her mind for help.

And the voice came again: "No help! Only you, alone. And me! And you will give in. You shall be mine!"

There was darkness then, for longer than she could remember. A sticky, slimy darkness that wrapped her round with pustulant tendrils as if some octopus of the night clutched her and sought to draw out her mind and soul through its slippery, invisible suckers.

And when that ended there was fire: she danced in a pit of flames, touching feet to coals that at first seemed cool so that she strode easily forwards until the coals glowed red and burned her feet so that she felt the pain and smelled the stink of her own burning flesh as she danced wildly, madly over the glowing pavement towards the end . . .

Which was a ladder of molten metal, its handrails and steps dripping into the smoke of the coals' fire.

She screamed and looked round for some other exit.

And there was a hand that thrust towards her, tempting, promising: relief.

She touched it and a voice said, "Mine."

She drew back, still screaming at the pain, and shouted, "No!"

And the voice assumed a face that was young and handsome and golden. And it said, "Yes."

And she looked at it. And felt her pain, and still said, "No."

Darkness.

Of light and hurting and thought. Darkness of remembered dreams and real pain. Of hate and love and memory: confusion.

Confusion.

Asleep or awake? The difference? Decide it: is there any difference?

She sank in a sea of molten metal. Tasted the sour odour of her own charring flesh melting from her burning bones. Saw the bubbling her skin made as it stripped clear of her limbs and plastered the surface of the red ocean with glistering pustules of flesh and fat and sinew.

She felt the pain.

And then there was ice: it came like a creeping flood of

blue-white nothingness that spanned the bare strictures of her flesh-bled limbs and coated the bones with freezing crystals of ice. The coldness extended along her limbs, filling the veins and the arteries with its chill until it climbed up into her mind, and froze that, also, all except a tiny part that cried out against the numbness and stayed hot and loyal.

And again she said, "No!"

And then there were spiders. Black and grey, putrescent green, with spindly legs that scuttled like shifting shadows over her body, their mandibles nipping skin as their poisonous tails bled numbing ichor into her body. She felt the scuttle and the darting of their nebulous, hairy legs over her breasts and eyes and mouth. Over the more secret parts of her body: and screamed:

"*No!*"

Then there were rats that nibbled at her eyelids and her toes. And snakes that writhed and curled about her, their warm scales as much a shock as the soft pattering of the rat's claws or the spiders' limbs.

She felt her feet and hands and eyes stripped from her; gave way to the pain of sundered flesh. Felt venom fill her veins and dripping spider's poison numb her body.

But still screamed, "No!"

And then it was ended, as if it had never been. She rested in a garden of clean-smelling trees, all ringed with bushes that wafted the scent of roses and hyacinths and tulips about her.

And she opened her eyes against the horror and saw beauty, and the golden-haired devil smiling at her with a cup of wine in his hand.

And he said, "Take it. It will make you feel better."

And she said, "No. I don't want it."

The creature smiled, shrugging. His hand opened, releasing the cup, which fell towards the grass. Then it was no longer there, flashing out of existence before it touched the sward. Raven ignored the display: such minor magic was common to any sorcerer's repertoire.

"Few people refuse me." His voice was gentle again, soothing. "It is not a thing I bear easily."

"Nor do I easily submit to abduction," Raven snarled. "Release me."

The creature laughed, a fluting, melodious sound that was somehow filled with menace.

"In this place it is I who command," he murmured, still gently. "Your desires mean nothing. You are powerless."

He lowered himself with fluid grace, stretching on the grass beside her. Smiling, he reached out to stroke a hand along her naked thigh. Raven had expected his flesh to have some different texture, remembering the black, charred-looking thing he had become in the room. Instead, it was soft and smooth, the touch caressing as the voice. The fingers traced a line across her belly, moving casually towards her womanhood like a lover's soft fondling.

She shuddered and drove her hand, fingers stiffened, at the throat. Trained by Argor in the savage arts of unarmed combat, her reflexes battle-honed, her thrust should have crushed the creature's windpipe—would have killed any mortal man. But the blow was stopped. There was no visible movement, but suddenly her hand was gripped as though in a vice. The man-thing went on smiling.

"You cannot defeat me, Raven. My strength is unimaginable to your petty little human mind. Do not fight me, for such opposition is pointless."

"What are you?" She fell back as he released his grip, rubbing at fingers numbed by his crushing fist. "Why do you taunt me?"

"What I am would have no meaning for you." He rested on one elbow, toying with a flower. "I come from a place far removed from the squabbling kingdoms that surround your Worldheart sea, a place as superior to your world as the Altan's palace to a herdsman's hut."

"Since you feel such contempt for my world, why do you trouble with it?"

The creature stared at the flower it was holding, then began to pluck away the petals, one by one; carefully.

"Because that is my nature. Perhaps I shall tell you a little of my world, that you may better understand the futility of opposing me." He looked up, amusement on his face. "I belong to a race older by far than your kind. The Ketta, we are called, and once we ruled this world for it amused us to watch the antics of you puppet-people. Once we ruled many worlds, and with such diversity of play-things we forgot this little dung-pile. When it pleased us to look at you again, we saw that you had grown somewhat. There was even a stirring of conscience evident, a sense of right.''

The last petal fell from the flower and the Ketta crushed the naked core between forefinger and thumb, an expression of distaste on his features.

''Such feelings do not please us, nor do the damnable machinations of Kharwhan. So I chose to return here, to end those machinations.''

''So Kharwhan is strong enough to defy you,'' Raven said quickly. ''You fear the Ghost Isle.''

For an instant there was a hint of the Ketta's other embodiment, as though anger disturbed its shape to reveal its true self.

''I fear nothing. Should I desire, I might destroy Kharwhan and all its mewling minions. Look!''

It gestured at a tree that stood nearby, the branches gnarled and sturdy. Flame blazed, engulfing the trunk, leaping out along the branches. There was a stink of burning, then only a wisp of smoke above a patch of blackened soil. The Ketta gestured again: grass sprouted, covering the charred earth, and a bush heavy with scarlet flowers stood there.

Raven feigned awe, realising that the creature was vain: that such weakness might prove useful to her.

''I fear nothing,'' it repeated. ''I merely choose to destroy the island slowly, to let the upstart sorcerers savour the gradual ruin of all they seek to build.''

''And how will you accomplish this aim?''

''Once, long and long ago by your reckoning, I chose to take the name of Vedast. I was worshipped as a god in the place you now call Xandrone.'' Laughter, ugly with madness, bubbled from the Ketta's lips. ''I shall return as that deity and summon my followers to a holy war. From Xandrone we shall spread about the rim of the ocean until Kharwhan stands alone, then, when the sorcerer-priests are able clearly to review their fate I shall crush them.''

He paused, smiling at Raven, who asked, "And I? What part do I play in this scheme?"

"That," chuckled the Ketta, "is the most pleasing part of all. Kharwhan chose you to further its designs, now I shall use you to destroy the island. You it was defeated the Altan's dream of empire; you who thwarted Belthis' vision of dominance; you who halted the Shadow Lords. Now I have chosen you. For you, Raven, shall lead my army against the Ghost Isle."

"Never!" The denial sprang instinctively to her lips. "I shall not!"

The pain returned, as if liquid fire filled her veins, as if her eyes boiled in her skull, her brain melted. She tasted fire, smelt the acrid scorching of her flesh. Screamed.

The pain abated and she was pinioned to a column of green marble. Manacles fettered her wrists, dragging her arms up high above her head so that her breasts jutted proudly forwards. Ankle rings held her legs spread wide, exposing all her body. Before her there shuffled ghastly, bestial monsters, the product of nightmare. Some resembled great apes with hunched, misshapen bodies and curving, saliva-dripping fangs. Others were as the Beastmen from the Ishkarian Rift, their bodies humanoid, but their features those of wolves or pigs or goats. Yet more seemed as men, but men with twisted features, sore-covered bodies that oozed pus and excrement, bone showing through the putrescent flesh as if they rotted before her horrified eyes.

The creatures shambled towards her, roaring and gibbering, toying obscenely with huge members, making obvious their intention.

This is not real, she told herself. *It cannot be.*

And the voice of the Ketta, the bellowing, thundering voice entered her mind, shouting.

It is real! I decree it so.

And the freaks moved in, arms that ended in talons, fingers of diseased bone reaching towards her. Touching. Stroking. An ape-thing, its back humped and covered with bristling hair, its eyes filled with writhing worms, thrust a paw between her legs, probing.

She screamed, "No!"
And the awful scene dissolved.

She was again in the garden, stretched upon the soft,
sweet-smelling grass, the scent of flowers in the air, the
song of birds trilling from the bushes. She trembled, wiping sweat from face and breasts, staring down at her
thighs, where droplets of blood marked the place of the
ape-beast's fumbling.

"Reality is what I wish it to be," remarked the Ketta;
casually, as though discussing some point of philosophy.
"I *can*, if I wish, subject you to such agony as will leave
you mad. I can destroy you as easily as I pluck a flower.
There is no denying me, Raven. You cannot defeat me or
oppose me. Not with sword or body or mind."

"But if you destroy me," she forced her body to cease
its trembling, fighting to control her voice, "then you
destroy your own purpose in taking me."

"You juggle words," smiled the golden-haired figure.
"And you do it badly. Should you outlive your usefulness,
then I shall discard you. I might empty your mind, render
you a golem, to do my bidding as I will it."

The thought of such a fate, reminding her as it did of
what Karl ir Donwayne had become, sent a fresh shiver of
horror through her mind. But accompanying the horror
was also a glimmer of hope, a faint, dim chance that was
borne out by the Ketta's next words.

"I should, of course, prefer that you obey me willingly.
To know that you fight against Kharwhan of your own
choice would render the game that much the sweeter."

He reached out to touch her again, cupping his hand
about her breast. She shuddered, but did not flinch from
his caress, knowing that her sole hope lay in dulling his
suspicions.

"Spellbinder will seek me," she said. "And he is a
mage of considerable power."

"And I," replied the Ketta, "am a god of infinite
power. Even should your puny wizard succeed in finding
you he would be unable to save you. He would find only
his own death."

The confidence with which he spoke chilled Raven,

prompting her to wonder how true his boasting might be. That he was immensely powerful was clear, though if that mystic strength he commanded was too forceful for even Spellbinder was a doubt that could be resolved in only one way. And for that resolution, it was necessary that the warrior-wizard locate her.

"Where are we?" she asked innocently. "In Xandrone still?"

"In limbo," came the answer. "Though the entry point is hidden in those hills you know as the World's End mountains. A suitable title, given my intentions."

"And if Spellbinder should succeed in finding that place?"

"Then he must overcome the guardians I have left there." The alien creature patted her cheek. "Do not waste time thinking of rescue: he will never pass those creatures posted at my door. Think instead of your own fate. I shall leave you a while to ponder thereon."

He rose, extending a hand to help her up. She accepted, glancing about her, and asked, "May I have clothing?"

"If you wish it," agreed her captor. "Though there is little need."

"I should feel easier," said Raven humbly. "Better able to think on your words."

"The foibles of humanity amaze me," smiled the Ketta. "What petty things you are. However, if it will help persuade you . . ."

He took her hand again and she felt a sudden disorientation, as though the ground shifted beneath her. For an eye's blink she was blind, whiteness dazzling her vision. When sight returned she was alone in a spacious chamber, wide doors opening on to a balcony, other doors opening in the three remaining walls. Swiftly she crossed to the balcony, her bare feet padding over smooth, slightly warm marble. There was a balustrade at waist height of the same material as the floor, green vines all thick with delicate flowers of red and yellow and purple twining about the intaglio work.

She leaned over the rim, wondering if the vines were strong enough to support her weight. Below her they crept down the wall, which was high, too high to risk a fall, ending where a narrow strip of grass bounded the foot.

There was a moat of translucent blue water, in which dark shapes moved lazily beneath the surface. She tested a vine. It broke in her hand: the thin tendrils were far too weak. She cursed softly, calculating the distance to the water. She might, she knew, manage the dive, and the farther bank was close enough for swimming. But the creatures in the water? It seemed unlikely the Ketta would leave unguarded so obvious an escape route.

As though to answer her wondering, one of the marine beasts rose to the surface. A sleek, narrow head set on a slender neck lifted into the air, baleful green eyes surveying the land. Jaws long as her arms opened to expose rows of gleaming, needle-pointed teeth. Then the beast dived, affording her a brief glimpse of a serpentine body, limbs tipped with hooked claws, a lashing, barbed tail.

She turned away, recognising the futility of that avenue.

She stared out across the moat. On the far bank the land ran down in a wide meadow almost a kli in width, ending at a great, wild forest that stretched away into misty blueness that was impenetrable to her gaze. She thought she detected movement along the edge of the woodland, but could not be certain, for when she attempted to probe the darkness of the trees it was still, brooding.

She concentrated on the building itself. To left and right the walls curved away, suggesting a tower. Above, the column rose towards a hazy sky of silvery blue, flecked across with drifting white clouds. The vines covered its surface, decking the place with a profusion of colour in which she saw windows, but no other balconies, though at the summit there appeared to be a cupola or dome of some kind, shimmering with a silver radiance that baffled the eye.

She returned inside, the faint warmth of hope cooling rapidly.

There was a table at the centre of the chamber, on it a decanter of carved glass and two silver goblets. A low couch and several deep chairs, all covered with some material she could not recognise, were set about the place. The walls were smooth and white, devoid of ornamentation other than a single, massive mirror in a simple frame of dark wood. She saw her own face reflected there, and remembered that she was naked.

The door facing the balcony was of the same ebon wood as the mirror's frame, plain save for a great brass handle. It refused to open when she tried it.

The second door slid silently wide, exposing a bedchamber. The floor was covered with thick, russet fur, warm beneath her feet. Tapestries of a golden-brown, velvety texture covered the walls except where a window let in light that added depth and dancing colour to the draperies. The window stood wide, twin frames of some clear crystal substance opening inwards. A massive bed occupied much of the space, a single fur of the same colour as that upon the floor covering its extremities. She noticed that the tapestries were drawn slightly back at one side, and found a secondary room, a large alcove equipped with a wardrobe and the kind of ornate dressing table she had seen in Karhsaam, though larger and finer than any there. Ignoring the perfumes and jewellery scattered across the surface, she went to the wardrobe. Inside, like some courtesan's dream, were gowns and robes, tunics, underclothing, slippers, all of exquisite design and such colour as would dim a rainbow.

Raven selected a plain shift of white silk, surmounting that with a gown of dark blue, the bodice hugging her figure and fastening high about her slender neck, the skirt long and swirling, slit on one side from ankle to thigh. The garment was circled at the waist by a narrow band of silver links, and there were slippers of a matching colour, set with tiny silver beads.

Dressed, but increasingly frustrated, she returned to the antechamber to investigate the third door.

There was a bathroom here, mirrored walls surrounding a gigantic sunken tub, beside which were arrayed perfumes and unguents and scented salts. She was reminded of the interview granted by Quez M'ystal, the Altan, in his opulent bathing chamber. But even that paled in comparison with the magnificence of the Ketta's creation.

A movement behind her ended the examination and she turned to see the Ketta watching her. He—for she found it difficult to think of him as a thing, as *it*—was changed into a shirt of black silk, loose-fitting, belted with a wide band of black leather. Tight black breeches covered his legs, tucked inside high boots of the same midnight hue.

He smiled and said, "You look magnificent. Such finery suits you well; better than war gear."

"But you would put me in war gear," answered Raven. "Where is my armour? My blade?"

"Safe. You have no need for such kit here." He gestured at the couch. "Come, sit down. Take some wine."

Raven obeyed, adjusting the folds of her gown so that her legs were hidden. The Ketta noticed, fixing his blank, blue stare on her face.

"You subscribe to me the emotions of men. Do you begin to think of me as human, then?"

"You appear so in shape. Why not in feeling?"

"To lust? Perhaps I do. But I am many things to many men. I am what I desire." He filled the goblets, bringing them over to the couch. "Do not concern yourself with that aspect. Not for now. In time, perhaps, you will come to me pleading for my favour."

Raven sipped the wine without replying.

"You have seen my power," continued the Ketta, "do not forget and there will be no further need of demonstration. Rather would I show what you might share."

Again Raven sensed that note of vanity in his voice, and thought to choose her words with care: too swift an acquiescence would be obvious. Just as she would test an enemy's swordskill in blade-fight, so she sought to probe the reserves of this opponent.

"What might I share?" she asked. "The destruction of the world I know?"

"Mayhap I should build a better one," smiled the Ketta. "In any event, surely it is better to live a spell in hope than know immediate death."

"Mayhap," she answered cautiously. "But this sharing you speak of, what is that?"

"Let us eat," he suggested, "and I will show you after."

His words reminded Raven that she was hungry. Until now she had not thought of food, such basic considerations driven from her mind by confusion and fear and rage.

Abruptly, she was reminded that her last meal had been the meagre prison fare offered by Haral's dungeon. Indeed, she was reminded that she had no idea how long she had been a prisoner of the Ketta: time lacked meaning in this magical domain.

The Ketta rose, offering his arm with a courtesy that was mocking in its politeness. He escorted her decorously to the exit, which opened at his touch as if no lock, either magical or mechanical, existed there. She found herself in a broad corridor, windowless but lit with a soft radiance that seemed to shine from the very fabric of walls and ceiling and floor. A little way on there was a door, the twin of that fronting her chambers. It opened at their approach and the Ketta ushered her through.

Beyond lay a banqueting hall of black and silver stone, its roof arched and spanned by carved buttresses, the walls set with intricate patterns of inlaid metal. A great fireplace, the hearth deep and tall, was built into one wall, logs piled, unlit, upon the flags. Before it stood a long table of polished wood, the legs carved in a menagerie of weird beasts, the same strange decorations wandering over the high-backed chairs that flanked the great trestle. High up, on the wall that faced the hearth, was a gigantic window of coloured glass. There was no visible joining of the colours, as if all were cast together in the one great expanse at a single melding. Light shone through, becoming transformed to a rainbow patterning that filled the hall with flickering luminescence, simultaneously soothing and confusing to the eye.

At one end of the table, two places were set. The Ketta led Raven to her seat with that same obscene correctitude, drawing back the chair and standing until she was settled.

An abundance of viands occupied the space between their plates, which Raven noticed were of beaten gold, meats and platters of fish, roasted birds and pies that wafted spicy odours to her nostrils, vegetables in steaming mounds, and fruit, cheeses, several kinds of bread. Flasks of wine, some the red of blood, others paler, as if tinted with rose petals, some white, or green, or yellow, stood beside goblets of crystal and gold and silver. There was sufficient provender for twenty hungry men set out, and

wine in quantity enough to render them all tipsy. Raven
wondered at the extravagance: was it for her sake alone
that her captor made such display?

"Allow me." The Ketta carved meat from a joint.
"This will, I trust, prove to your liking."

It did; the meat was succulent, with a flavour she could
not recognise, the vegetables crisp and fresh-tasting, both
savoury and sweet.

She saw that he, too, ate with gusto, and again wondered at his nature. If the human form he assumed was
possessed of normal human appetites, then surely it must
equally be subject to ordinary human weaknesses. For a
moment she thought of turning her knife on him, but then
recalled the speed with which he had blocked her earlier
attack. No, she decided, better to wait, study him until
such time as she might be more certain of his vulnerabili-
ties and turn them positively to her advantage.

Throughout the meal the Ketta maintained a flow of
casual conversation, always attentive to her needs, playing
the part of benevolent host rather than threatening captor.
And Raven, in turn, acted a role, that of prisoner-guest,
becoming gradually accustomed to her position, resigned
to her fate.

When they were finished eating, he pushed back his
chair.

"If you are ready, I will fulfill my promise. In part, at
least."

Although he smiled as he said it, and his tone was
smooth as ever, there remained the unmistakable hint of
menace in his words. Raven hid a shudder behind a nervous smile and rose to her feet.

They quit the hall and followed the corridor to a low-
arched entrance from which a spiral stairway wound upwards. The Ketta led the way, cautioning Raven against
the steepness of the ascent and halting at intervals to
enquire if she was wearied, would like to rest. She hid her
irritation, trusting that such solicitude indicated an assump-
tion of feminine weakness rather than some subtle mockery.

How far they climbed and how long it took she could
not guess. The constant turning dizzied her, combining
with the unreality of the place to render time and distance

meaningless. It was as the Ketta had said: they existed in limbo.

At last, as her calves and soles really began to ache with the effort, the staircase disgorged on a circular chamber barely large enough to accommodate them both. A door of black metal, curved to fit snug against the wall, faced them. The Ketta pressed his right palm to the surface, murmuring in a voice too low for Raven to catch the words, and the door swung open; he stepped back, motioning for Raven to enter first.

They were, she guessed, inside the cupola visible from her balcony, though what distortion of space rendered the climb so long, she could not imagine. The room was circular, surrounding the central core formed by the stairhead. Around the inner wall ran a flat, black shelf, its surface covered with multi-faceted, many-coloured discs she assumed were jewels. At intervals, beneath the shelf, there were deep, heavily padded chairs with high backs and thick arms. The floor, she noticed, was black, too, and yielding to her steps, slightly spongy. The outer wall, joining the roof in an unbroken curve that rendered differentiation between wall and ceiling meaningless, was of an opaque, milky white, its texture cool and hard against her fingers.

The Ketta paused beside the door, studying the strange black shelf as if admiring the myriad hues of the jewels. Raven waited, intrigued despite her misgivings. The being ignored her, his politeness momentarily forgotten as he paced slowly around the chamber, blue eyes fixed intently on the sparkling lights.

Finally he looked up, smiling, and pointed at the outer wall.

"Watch."

Raven turned, not knowing what it was she should look for.

Slowly, as the muddied surface of a clear pool loses its opacity as the submarine disturbance dies, the milkiness drained away. Wall and ceiling became transparent, and Raven found herself standing, so it seemed, on air, floating in the blue sky. Involuntarily, she gasped and stepped back from that great, blue emptiness.

The Ketta's hands clutched her shoulders, and for the first time she was grateful for his touch: the contact restored a degree of reality.

"Watch," he said again, his voice gentle in her ear. "And I will show you what you might share."

Ten

*"If you have no map, then you must seek a landmark.
The wise traveller is never truly lost."*

Xand Rider's saying.

Spellbinder reined in and lifted his waterbag from the
saddle. The contents were tepid and tasted faintly of leather,
but the liquid refreshed him somewhat, removing the furred
parchness from his mouth.

To his left, Gondar Lifebane wiped a hand over his
beard and said, "By the Mother, friend! How much farther? My body's built for sea travel, not this numb-arsed
journeying."

"The oracle should be in sight come morning." Despite
his concern for Raven, Spellbinder could not help smiling
at the reiver's complaints. "You can soak those parts that
pain you then."

"I'd need a tub for a day," grumbled the Lifebane.
"And a maiden with a bucket of salve to minister my
wants."

"We'd best camp at full dark," suggested Argor. "The
horses are hard pressed to maintain this pace."

Spellbinder nodded agreement. "We'll find a likely place
and move on at sun's rise."

They kicked the tired animals to a slow canter, pushing
on across a landscape empty of feature other than the
seemingly endless grass. From time to time they passed
herds of Xand browsing on the rich summer forage, and
the great beasts would lift their shaggy heads and watch
the three men ride past, the bulls moving instinctively to
form a screen between cows and horsemen. The sun lowered, its clear brilliance becoming first yellow, then tinged
with pink, and finally red. Behind them a pale moon grew
visible and overhead a skein of homing birds lilted a
farewell to the day.

114

They halted when the moon was high and built a fire over which they cooked the last of their provisions. Somewhere in the darkness a hunting beast howled, and was answered by the challenging bellow of a Xand. The three travellers wrapped themselves in their cloaks and slept with weapons close to hand.

They woke at dawn and mounted again, moving steadily westwards in the direction of Srygar.

As the sun began to heat the dew-moist grass, raising a damp, enveloping mist, they came to the place of the oracle. It was, in miniature, like the Ishkarian Rift, and had there not been the sound of voices and thin columns of smoke to warn them, they might easily have plunged into the gap that opened like a wound in the plain. Running directly across their path was a cut, its sides grey stone against the green. A narrow trail sloped downwards to a meadow two kli or more wide, a thin stream gleaming at its centre. A straggle of tents ran alongside the water, the occupants emerging to study the newcomers with dark, suspicious eyes. Several men began to move surreptitiously towards the riding Xands penned behind the tents, scimitars and throwing stars in their hands.

"We come in peace." Spellbinder used the Xandronian tongue. "Travellers come to consult the oracle."

"Why would outlanders seek the oracle of Ban?" demanded a dark, thick-bearded fellow with a bandage about his left shoulder. "The seer concerns herself only with the affairs of Xandrone."

"It is of such matters we would speak," replied Spellbinder calmly.

"It is not usual," said the wounded man stubbornly. "Why would outlanders dabble in our affairs? Unless you be outlaws, seeking loot."

Gondar, who understood sufficient of the dialect to follow the exchange, spat and loosened his great axe where it hung between his shoulders. He said, "If that were our purpose we'd not seek riches in this midden."

The Xandronian glared and raised the scimitar he carried.

"Step down from that spindly animal you ride, whorespawn!" His voice was harsh, furious. "We'll see how your bones grace our midden."

Gondar snarled in turn and loosened his feet in the stirrups. Argor reached quickly to grasp the reiver's hand as it closed upon the axe haft, murmuring, "Hold, Lifebane. Be patient, lest you lose us Raven before we find her."

Spellbinder said, "Peace, peace. We are not outlaws, friend, only wanderers, as I told you. We come questing for a friend, with reason to believe that only the oracle of Ban may inform us of her whereabouts."

The bandaged man continued to glare, but his arm relaxed a little so that the curved blade pointed at the ground again.

"I am Gall ta Kereth, champion of the Vanna clan," he said. "In Haral I slew the best they sent against me. I won the Horns. I leave death behind me and I take insult from no man."

"No insult was meant," said Spellbinder, swiftly; placatingly. "My companion is of Kragg, where tempers run hot and swift. He is unused to the ways of Xandrone. He will apologise to the champion of the Vanna clan, whose skill with blade and beast is truly mighty. I know this, for I saw you fight in Haral."

Gall ta Kereth was further mollified by this praise, and his rage abated. But still he insisted that Gondar apologise.

The golden-haired giant chewed his beard, muttering in his own language, "Must the Lifebane now crawl to grassgrubbers?"

"Aye, he must," said Argor, "for if he looks about him he will see that we are ringed round by armed men who will leave our carcasses to feed the grass if he refuses. Think on Raven, man! Think on our quest!"

"Oh, Raven, Raven!" grumbled the reiver. "I'd give my life for you. Must I sell my honour, too?"

"Aye," said Spellbinder. "And swiftly. Before it all bleeds away on the point of a lance."

Gondar moaned and stared down at Gall ta Kereth. "I ask your pardon," he said. "I spoke in haste, not seeing how lovely is your pleasant valley."

The clansman nodded, satisfied. "I accept your apology, stranger. Climb down and share food with me. I will send a man to ask audience of the seer."

Swiftly, anxious to avoid any further delay, Spellbinder

dismounted. Argor, and then Gondar, followed suit. Ta Kereth led them inside the tent, inviting them to settle on the furs covering the floor while a woman set to preparing food.

"I had thought the Vanna clan herded on the western boundary," said Spellbinder, controlling the conversation for fear Gondar might spoil the truce. "Close against the mountains."

"That is true," nodded their host. "We ride that part shadowed by the World's End mountains, and I shall go there soon. I took a scratch in the combats and quit Haral to rest here. I have no great love of cities, and on the coast there is overmuch talk of the Lord Vedast. His minions buzz about like flies on a dung-pile, seeking to convert all to his following."

"I had believed Vedast to be popular." Spellbinder hid his excitement. "I understood his following grew apace."

"So it does." Ta Kereth flicked his left wrist, two fingers extended in a dismissive gesture. "So does a grass fire. And both promise death."

"You have no liking, then, for Vedast's new strength?" Spellbinder prompted.

"His strength lies mainly in the cities," came the answer, "where there is not enough room. The city folk are so crowded together they seek to extend their boundaries. Vedast—or his priests—promise them a world. We of the Vanna have all the world we need here on the grass. If the Horn God intended us to have more he would call Alaria, his bride, to seed other lands with such sproutings as our Xands might eat. As things are, our beasts can live only in Xandrone, or on such fodder as we send abroad."

The basic logic of the explanation settled the matter in his mind, and he applied himself to his food in such a way that Spellbinder deemed it wiser to let the subject drop.

For a while they ate in silence, then a man appeared at the entrance of the tent to announce the readiness of the seer. Spellbinder rose and followed him, telling his two companions to wait.

The oracle of Ban was unadorned, no sign or symbol announcing its existence, merely a small, dark hole in the grey rock of the cleft. The hole was barely large enough to

permit a child entry, and the warrior-wizard was forced to
crawl along a dark tunnel like some earth-burrowing animal. The tunnel opened on a cave, lit dimly by the red
glow of a small fire. It was unpleasantly warm there, the
atmosphere sticky and redolent of decay.

Spellbinder squatted on the floor, waiting.

The fire crackled, growing brighter, and its light showed
others sitting about the chamber, silent and grey; unmoving. As the light grew, Spellbinder saw that the silent
figures would never move: all were dead, corpses of various ages. Many were little more than dust, bound up in the
preserving burial robes; other were skeletal; the more recent yet preserved fragments of flesh upon their bones,
from which came the odour.

"You sit in honourable company, outlander." The voice
was dry, amused. "For these are my predecessors, the
seers of Ban down all the lonely ages. They saw much in
their time, and now they have passed their knowledge on
to me, one from one to one. Think on that, stranger: all
that knowledge."

The fire died before he could see clearly from which
shrouded figure the voice came, and none moved to grant
him clue. He waited in the gloomy shadow for the seer to
speak again.

"What would you ask?" The chamber, he realised, was
carved so as to distort sound, the whispering echoes render-
ing impossible any identification of the speaker. "I may
help you."

"There is an evil abroad in Xandrone. It is, I believe,
linked to this fresh worshipping of Vedast. A thing connected to it took my companion, Raven. I believe it lairs to
the west, in the mountains. I would know where, and how
I may find it. And her."

There was silence again, and the fire dimmed as though
the life was sucked from it, leaving only ashes.

Then: "You are of Kharwhan."

"Aye," he said. "I am."

"We know of Raven." The whispering seemed to emanate from all the mummies at once, like a chorus.
"Swordmistress of Chaos. World-changer. She may yet
die."

"But now she lives?" He risked the interruption in his excitement. "You know that?"

"We know that. We know all." The rustling grew louder: "Vedast is evil. He would drive my people down into ruin. He would tear down all the world. The mad god is ambitious."

Again, that dark, malodorous silence. Spellbinder pinched in his nostrils against the stink and waited.

"It will not be easy. Vedast is strong. You may lose more than your life. Will you chance such loss?"

"I and my companions," he answered firmly. "Readily."

"We have heard brave words before. And known them to turn to fear-piss when confronted with the truth."

He sensed a reply was called for, and said: "With me ride Argor and Gondar Lifebane. We are pledged to seek Raven and destroy this evil. If die we must, then so it goes."

"A warrior-mage, an outlaw mercenary, and a sea-reiver. Mayhap you can succeed: I sense a power in you." There came then a rustling like wind through rotted leaves; he recognised it as laughter. "Aye, mayhap you can. But you will need more help than mine. You will need Gall ta Kereth for a guide and passport to where you must go. Him and that black creature, the guardian of Kharwhan; the bird."

Once more silence filled the chamber. Once more Spellbinder fought impatience, sitting quiet until the seer spoke again. This time the voice was lifted in a sing-song chant.

"You must go where none can pass,
Where death's drear stone divides the grass.
Where sun and light and all life dies,
And corpses rot beneath the skies,
That once were blue.
Tread in fear where eyes are blind
And death's dread demons stalk behind.
Beware the blade of foe and friend,
For life must cease before you end,
This journey."

The chanting ceased, whispering into nothingness on the final words. Bright flame spouted from the embers, illuminating empty eye sockets, grinning yellow teeth, fleshless faces. Spellbinder blinked, dazzled by the sudden brilliance.

"Go now, Spellbinder. We have told you all we can. Send Gall ta Kereth here. Speak to no one of this until word comes to you."

"My thanks." He rose, ducking beneath the low roof.

"Destroy Vedast, if you can. That is all the thanks we ask."

He nodded and crawled into the tunnel, glad to be gone from the corpse-stink of the place. Gladder still that he had gone there.

Outside, the mist had cleared and the sun shone into the valley. He shaded his face, letting his vision adjust to the day's brightness, conscious of the staring, curious eyes that followed him as he paced slowly back to the tent. He passed the seer's command to Gall ta Kereth, who hurried to obey for all a look of worry dimmed his smile, and sat down.

Instantly Gondar and Argor demanded knowledge of the oracle's message.

"A riddle," he told them. "That and a warning. I cannot tell you."

"By the Mother!" Gondar slapped irritably at his sheathed sword. "Seers and oracles and prophets shroud themselves in more mystery than a Lyand whore. Strip the veils from the girl and you find a hag with her youth painted on her face: the mystery fades fast as the desire."

"But the coins still clink as readily the next time," smiled Argor. "For the mystery remains and men live ever in hope."

"No payment was asked," murmured Spellbinder thoughtfully. "And oracles are known to speak the truth. It is for us to unravel the mystery."

"It is all we have," Argor nodded sombrely. "If silence was demanded, let it be so, lest we blight our hopes of finding Raven."

"It is good to know you heed the seer." Gall ta Kereth spoke from the tent's mouth. "For that was a test of your faith."

"By all the gods of sea and sky!" roared Gondar. "First is my temper tested, and now my trust."

"Faith is a powerful weapon," said Spellbinder. "Calm your pride, old friend, and hear what ta Kereth has to say."

The Vanna man hunkered to the furs, his brow furrowed.

"I am to lead you to my clan," he said. "To our holding by the mountains. Until then you must speak to no one of the message. At that time you will receive word, and only then are you to speak."

"And how shall we receive this word?" demanded Gondar. "What message will bring it?"

"I know not," shrugged ta Kereth. "Only what the oracle told me."

"Perhaps the bird," suggested Argor calmly. "It has proven its worth before."

"Aye, you speak the truth." Gondar regretted his impatience. "I am in a fret to be moving, to seek out Raven."

"Then let us depart." Gall ta Kereth rose, grinning now. "To speed our going the seer has full healed my wound, and the day grows old as we sit here talking."

"I might come to call this herdsman a friend," said Gondar, endangering the tent as he sprang to his full height. "Aye, that I might."

"And I might allow you," said the clansman. "When I know you worth it."

The Lifebane stared open-mouthed for a moment, lost for words. Then he bellowed a laugh that echoed about the valley and slapped a hand against ta Kereth's shoulder that rocked the smaller man back on his heels.

"We'll fight over that privilege later," he chuckled. "If we still feel the need."

The champion of the Summer Gathering laughed in turn, staring up at the lord of Kragg. "Come, let's be riding," he said. "Friend."

Eleven

"Words may be soft and wine may be sweet, and both
may hide poison. It is the source that is important."
                                    The Books of Kharwhan.

Beneath the tower, like a sea of green and grey and blue
and black, the forest spread in all directions. No trails
were visible, nor any clearings. There was no discernible
ending to the ocean of dark foliage, only that strange,
far-away shimmer that baffled the eye, adding to the sense
of vastness, of loneliness.

"All I see are trees," said Raven. "Nothing more."

"Watch," said Ketta.

The light danced, as if sun reflected momentarily from
some bright surface just out of her range of vision, then
the blueness at the forest's rim seemed to roil, like wind-
stirred fog. And then, though she could still see no movement other than that distant stirring, it was all about her,
hiding everything.

She began to turn, but the Ketta's hand grasped her
shoulder and held her still.

"Watch," he repeated.

And she was looking down as might an eagle, looking
over a vast expanse of grass. Though she had never seen
the plains of Xandrone she knew this enormity of green
must be those. And then she saw a shadow creeping over
the green; a great dark shifting, as if the ocean rolled in to
swamp the land. Her vision drew closer, and she became
aware of a rumbling, sullen thunder, as if all the greatest
drums ever beaten were struck at once. And she saw
beneath her a horde such as the world had never known.
Shaggy Xands, horns tossing swept, flood-like, inexora-
ble, over the grass. Men rode the beasts, flaunting lances
and shields, scimitars flashing bright. Amongst them were
wagons, great creaking vehicles that bore siege catapults,

122

onagers, arbalests; more that were covered over with canvas; and still more open, piled with weapons and armour and supplies.

The movement of the horde shook the earth, for it spread into the distance as far as she could see. And she saw amongst the Xands and the wagons marching squadrons of black-skinned men, the warriors of Sly, armed with bows and great spears with blades like palm leaves, bright feathers in their hair, their eyes wide and white against the darkness of their flesh.

And Beastmen from Ishkar, bearing ancient swords and sharp-pointed staves; or no weapons at all, other than their fangs and claws and tusks and horns.

And over the groaning, creaking, rumbling thunder of the horde there rose a shouting like the tumult of a storm-tossed sea beating against rock.

"Vedast! *Vedast!* VEDAST!"

And: "Raven! *Raven!* RAVEN!"

And she saw herself, mounted astride a huge black Xand, its horns clad in silver, its eyes red, teeth champing, saliva dripping. She wore her armour of black mail, her hair streaming free, the gem-hilted sword aloft in her hand.

And she led the horde, bright-eyed and proud as she heard the roaring behind her.

"Raven!"

"*Raven!*"

"RAVEN!"

It was as though the earth itself shouted, the thunder bellowing from the bowels of the world, deafening, numbing.

She pressed hands to her ears and closed her eyes.

And when she opened them again there was a city. Ruined, with smoke wafting from burning towers and blazing houses, the stones torn down, the timber charred and black. And the streets were red and the air was filled with the stink of blood and fire.

And there was another place, a sea port by the look, for the ocean lapped against slimed walls of green stone. Though few walls stood, and where they did the roofs were gone, smashed in by catapults and fire. The masts of ships poked up through the waves, and broken hulls dotted the shoreline. Bodies, white from the water, and swollen, nibbled at by fishes, floated on the swell.

And the sea was red, the scarlet of fire reflected from the crimson of blood. And carrion birds hung above the place, or stalked through the streets; feeding.

And there was a battlefield where the bodies still trembled as the ground shook at the horde's departure, and pariah dogs munched bones and fought over scraps of flesh.

And she saw Karhsaam in all its splendour, ringed round by the horde, besieged. And at the centre of the great camp stood a scarlet pavilion, all decked with gold and silver, and above it a banner flapped in the wind. And the banner was scarlet, with a black, gape-beaked bird emblazoned at the centre.

Catapults and onagers clashed, hurling rocks and blazing pitch at the city. Arbalests thrummed, driving massive shafts in whistling arcs through the smoky air. And the walls of Karhsaam fell and the horde streamed in, shouting, screaming its battle-cry:

"Raven! Vedast! Raven! Vedast!"

She sat amongst the wreckage of the Altan's palace, her armour slick with blood, her sword across her thighs, crimson dripping from the blade. At her feet lay the body of Quez M'yrstal; beside it, that of his sister-wife, Krya. And she was laughing as her warriors tossed the two heads high in the air. And beside her, smiling, was the Ketta.

And she saw Quwhom, its blue ice dark with blood. The towers of lovely Tywah smashed down, dull beneath a pall of smoke, the streets a charnel house through which roamed gleevahs and charga and tsabeen.

And there was the Obsidian Tower, no longer tall and proud, but a moss-grown rubble . . . The wooden fortresses of the Tribal Kingdoms burning, the fierce, proud warriors, from whose stock had come lost, dead Silver, ridden down by Xand-mounted soldiers, torn asunder by Beastmen, speared by Sly's cannibals.

And Kragg, smoke billowing sullen from Gondar's keep, the fields stark, poisoned with salt, the wolf-boats ablaze on a bloody sea, the reivers given over to the crows and the fishes.

*   *   *

She struggled against nausea, foulness clogging her
throat and tears blinding her eyes, so that her voice was
low, husky as she cried out, "No! No more! I cannot bear
it!"

"You must. You will." The Ketta's voice had lost its
gentle tone now; become gloating, filled with an obscene,
horrible excitement. "There is more. Watch!"

She tried to turn, but found some force—not his hands—
holding her still. She tried to shut her eyes, but could not,
and when she sought to raise her hands to cover her face,
they were gripped rigid by her sides.

And the shouting came back; dinning, remorseless,
deafening.

And she was standing in a golden chariot drawn by two
Xands, both black as night with silvered horns and scarlet
harness. Over the chariot fluttered the raven banner, but
now its pole was surmounted by a head. The sightless eyes
were blue, the colour of a summer sky when the sun beats
hot enough to bleach the azure from the heavens so that
they appear almost silver. The hair was black and long,
waving in the wind of the chariot's passage. The mouth
gaped wide, all bloody. And the blood dripped on her
face, and she licked at it, laughing.

And she heard her own voice say, "So it goes, Spellbinder."

And in the chariot, standing beside her, the Ketta laughed
and kissed the blood from her lips.

Then, as if her mind could no longer bear the agony of
the Ketta's visions, a darkness fell upon her. She gave
herself up to it, like some wounded animal creeping grace-
fully into a burrow, seeking respite; safety. She was dimly
aware of the Ketta's furious shout, of the force that still
held her upright seeking to jam open her eyes, unblock her
ears. But the darkness was stronger and swept her away.

As it did, she was conscious of a thought whispering in
her mind like a night wind, almost too faint to hear, barely
making itself known.

There is escape. His power can be stopped.

*   *   *

She woke. And with waking came memory: she rolled
on her side, spilling vomit across the fur-covered bed, her
body trembling, the horror of what she had seen racking
her, shaking her with great, heaving spasms.

When she was done and her stomach emptied, she rose.
She was naked, fouled with her own outpouring. She went
to the window, sucking in deep breaths to clear her head.
When she felt capable of further movement she went into
the bath-chamber and lowered herself thankfully into the
water, scrubbing at her arms and breasts and belly, rinsing
her hair until she felt clean again. Externally. Within her
there remained a tight knot of sickness as though the
images shown her had left some permanent taint. It was as
if the Ketta had revealed to her some dark and secret part
of her mind, a part so deeply suppressed that it was
forgotten; a part that might enjoy such power as her vision-
self had wielded, might perpetrate such horrors.

And at the same time it was a part the Ketta might bring
to the fore. She remembered his threats: that if pain and
persuasion failed he would mould her mind to his own
patterning.

She determined to die first.

Should escape prove impossible; should she be unable to
trick the alien creature; should Spellbinder fail to seek her
out—or fail to save her; then she would kill herself. She
drained the great tub and filled it afresh, thinking on the
ways such a design might be accomplished. In the Ketta's
presence, she suspected, it would be impossible. But there
was the balcony and the swimming horrors of the moat:
that might well be the way.

She rose from the water and dried herself, wandering
absently to the outer room. Crossing to the balcony she
saw darkness. Not the falling of night, but a total absence
of light as if some miasmic blanket was drawn about her
surroundings. The forest, even the moat below, was gone.
The walls of the tower were indistinct, nebulous: looking
up, she could no longer see the glistening dome. Nor was
there any sound. She stood, straining to hear some familiar
night noise, the rustle of a breeze through leaves or the
splash of water. But all was silent.

It was oppressive. As though the darkness and the absence of sound pressed in upon her with physical presence. The exit door remained immovable and she went into the bed-chamber, busying herself with her toilet in an attempt to ignore the weird stillness.

It was difficult, for even in the most tranquil places there is sound. In a tower such as this, were it normal, there should have been noise at any hour: the grumble of settling stone, the creak of wood cooling, footsteps, doors closing, voices; something. There was nothing.

She combed her hair and turned to the wardrobe. To her amazement she found her armour set out alongside the robes. The short-hemmed, heavy shift that would protect her body from the chafing of metal; the mail shirt; the high, metal-studded boots of Yr leather; the sleeve-shield; sword belt, with dirk and Tirwand blade scabbarded thereon; the wider belt, heavy with throwing stars. All were there.

Swiftly, comforted by the familiarity of the gear, she dressed, wondering what purpose the Ketta might have in arming her.

Accoutred, she returned to the outer room and drank a glass of wine, anticipating a visit from her captor.

He failed to come, and after a while she stretched on the bed, still dressed, and gave herself over to sleep. When she woke the sky was light again and food set out on the table in the antechamber. She satisfied her hunger and waited. Continued to wait until the darkness came again. Then slept.

And again she woke to brightness and food, which seemed to satisfy her for the whole period between waking and sleeping. And still the Ketta did not appear.

So it went on for a time she was unable to calculate. Whether the Ketta adjusted the periods of light and darkness to fit with a normal day, or whether they were adjusted to his whims, she could not tell. She assumed that he sought to break her will by isolating her, and devised routines to occupy her time and her mind.

On waking, she bathed, then ate half the food provided. After that she exercised, followed by a period of weapon training and a second bath to wash the sweat from her body. She ate again, then slept.

It was not enough.

She examined the rooms in minute detail. Tried on each garment in the wardrobe. Experimented with the perfume set out there. She sang every song she could recall, then forced herself to remember the words of half-forgotten tunes. She lay, eyes closed, remembering her past.

In time she found herself holding imaginary conversations with the non-existent Spellbinder and thought she must be driven mad.

And then she wept and the Ketta showed himself again.

She had fallen asleep in her armour, tears in her eyes.

She woke in a sun-dappled glade, all breeze-rustled foliage and dancing patterns of light and shadow. There was the scent of leaves and sweet-smelling grass, the gentle song of birds.

She lay upon the grass, and it was soft and warm and clean. The Ketta sat cross-legged beside her, dressed now in scarlet tunic and breeks the colour of oak leaves. He smiled as he watched her.

"Were you bored?"

The banality of the question struck her at first as amusing, but then she realised its truth and nodded; angrily.

"Imagine an eternity of such confinement. Never to speak to anyone; no book to read; nothing to see except those same, familiar views." His voice was soft, insinuating. "Your chamber might be smaller, even. Could you stand that?"

"I should go mad," she said, knowing it was the truth.

"But I might hold you sane. Hold you for ever in that limbo."

"I should kill myself." She said it firmly, meaning it. "Know that."

"I know you would try." He laughed now, taunting her. "But I should not permit you that escape."

"Do you govern death, then?" Raven asked. "That, surely, is the one inescapable fact that comes to all."

"I *am* death," smiled the Ketta. "Had you not realised that? You might refine your torments somewhat. You might open your wrists, or hurl yourself from the balcony, and then you *would* die. But I should bring you back to life each time. Think on that, my Raven. Think on that blade slicing your flesh. The hot, red blood and the warm, welcoming end. Then to wake and find yourself in the room again, all as before. Exactly as before.''

For an instant, though only for that brief fraction of time, she contemplated suicide there and then. The dirk was sheathed at her waist, one swift movement could have the blade out and driving upwards into her skull, into the brain. She dismissed the thought: it was not in her nature. And besides, she still held hope of defeating the creature.

Another thought crossed her mind. She was armoured: mayhap she could take the Ketta. Plant her sword in his heart and spill his guts about his feet.

As though sensing her contemplation, the Ketta said, ''You cannot kill me, Raven. I let you try once to teach you that.''

She nodded without speaking, staring at the woods and the grass as a thirst-tormented man might stare at cool water. And a great calm descended on her and she remembered two things.

The first was the way in which the visions had ended. There had come a point beyond which the Ketta was unable to control her, therefore his power *was* limited.

The second was of the nature of the images. The Ketta had been present only towards the end: that awful horde had followed her. Therefore she *was* necessary to his plans—or his pride—and he must prefer, as he had said, to have her conscious, if unwilling, co-operation.

So: if she was able to retain her sanity there must be hope. Perhaps if she appeared to give in she might be returned to the world, in which case Spellbinder would find her, and together they would fight the monster who claimed to be death.

And the Ketta himself gave her further hope, for he asked why she was so silent.

''I was enjoying the forest,'' she replied, thinking: *He cannot read my mind, he only guesses*. ''And I am hungry.''

''Forgive me.'' Again he was all courtesy. ''I will bring you food.''

He gestured at a point across the clearing, murmuring in a language she could not understand. A table of rough-hewn wood, suitable to the rustic setting, appeared in a shimmer of light, two chairs, and comestibles on earthenware platters. The Ketta rose, and Raven let him help her to her feet. They went to the table.

"You have told me what you intend to do." Raven spoke between mouthfuls, for she was truly hungry. "And shown me how you will achieve it."

"You now say *will*, rather than *may*," interrupted the golden-featured being. "Does this indicate some change in your position?"

"Perhaps," shrugged the woman, "you have made obvious your power. Clearly, I cannot resist you. At least, not without knowing madness or oblivion. And I have little wish to become a golem."

The Ketta smiled at her flattery.

"What you have shown me," Raven continued, pressing her advantage, "suggests that even Kharwhan must fall before your strength."

"*Will* fall," he corrected. "Inevitably and eternally."

"Will fall," she amended, smiling at him. "But what then? What of the horde? What of me? Shall I lead your armies into battle and then be cast off when my usefulness is ended? Such would be poor pay for a mercenary."

The Ketta smiled in turn, toying with a fruit.

"Those who aid me are rewarded." He bit into the fruit, ignoring the juice that ran down his jaw. "And those who seek to trick me suffer."

Raven felt a sudden chill sweep through her, and knew a moment of pure panic. Perhaps she was wrong. Perhaps he could read her mind, and was all the time playing with her. But she kept her face still, choosing to trust in her intuition and act out the game to the end. No matter what the consequences.

"Surely you know," she murmured humbly, "whether or not I seek to trick you."

"Of course," came the answer. "I make the point simply to remind you. In case you should, at some later time, consider betraying me."

"You have shown me what would happen." Raven shuddered, not feigning the distaste. "But what of the rewards?"

"Come." The Ketta stood up. Take my hand, and I will show you."

She rose, extending her arm to his grip. Again there was that cessation of existence, the momentary blankness, and then they stood in the corridor at the foot of the spiral stairs.

This time Raven was glad of the duration of the climb, for it allowed her a space in which to order her thoughts. Another weakness in the Ketta's armour was now apparent: although he seemed able to create illusion at will and transport them both through space, it seemed he could enter the chamber of illusions only by physical action. And some instinct told her that this strange room was integral to his power, a vital key.

Inside, whilst she fought the horror of memory, he turned again to the shelf of brilliant jewels. Again the blue mist rolled in, the blackness clearing to afford vicarious knowledge of possibilities, of what might be.

She sat upon a golden throne, bejewelled, her robe rich with precious stones. Rings encircled her fingers, necklaces hung about her shoulders, bracelets sparkled on her wrists. Beside her was the Ketta, smiling at the throng of courtiers milling about the sumptuous hall over which they presided.

Great was the hall, and splendidly decorated with tapestries and statuary and plates of carved and beaten metal, all of incalculable worth. The courtiers brought gifts of equal value, jewels and pearls, rare animals, weapons, ornate armour and costly clothes. It was such an array as the world had never seen, as would have ransomed a world. And the image-Raven laughed, for she knew it represented only a small part of her treasures.

And she was mounted on a superb horse, a great stallion, his coat gleaming black, caparisoned in scarlet and silver. She rode over meadows, splashing through streams, galloping down leafy woodland glades. And wherever she encountered people they cheered her, waving and bowing as she thundered by.

Then she was on the deck of a silver boat, its gleaming prow cutting blue water that sparkled and danced with the reflected magnificence of the vessel. The sails were scarlet, each one bearing the bird emblem, and the rigging was of woven gold, the fitments of jet, the anchors huge chunks of carved amber.

She stood at the stern, on planks of jade, sipping wine from a goblet of amethyst. And gulls wheeled above her while fishes sported in the sea, and the cries of the birds made her name echo in the wind. And beside her was the Ketta.

Then she was on a mountain, grey rock streaked through with black and gold; bare, windswept. She wore her armour here, and the wind made a streaming golden banner of her hair, stung her face. Close by, a torrent swept from the rock, cascading down and down in a spill of foaming white, its spray blown against her face and arms and thighs. And she laughed as she looked out over the fields below, over the farms and the cities and the far, far distant shore, for she knew that all belonged to her. That she could take whatever she chose, that none would deny her. For she was Raven, Swordmistress of Chaos; Mistress of the World.

And she was in darkness, a foetal vacuum of light-sprinkled black. She floated, a mote of life in the void, watching, waiting.

And light blazed before her, the near-unbearable radiance of suns, too distant to see clearly, that whirled in great spirals of myriad colours, kaleidoscopes that spun across the heavens. Whole worlds passed before her. Worlds of ice and worlds of water; worlds that were all volcanic rock, with molten seas and burning air; worlds that were green and lush with forests; worlds empty of inhabitants and worlds filled with people.

She saw buildings she could not believe; metal creations that flew like birds: and chariots that rolled without horse or Xand to draw them.

And then she was in the chamber once more, standing wide-eyed before the window that looked out over the now-familiar forest, her mind numb from those visions created by the Ketta's magic.

And the creature spoke softly, close behind her.

"That is what I could offer you." His voice, now, was smooth as honey, sweet as Saran wine. "All of that might be yours."

"If I lead your armies," she said softly.

"Yes. It seems a small price to pay for what I offer."

He set his hands upon her shoulders, turning her gently to face him. His featureless blue eyes stared into hers, his lips smiling, his voice softly insistent; beguiling.

"All that, Raven. All that and more. More than you could dream of in a thousand lifetimes. Does the reward not tempt you?"

"Yes," she said, returning his gaze. "Yes. It is very tempting."

Twelve

"If all the legions of the dead were raised, where should there be space for the living?"

Attributed to the Horn God.

Srygar faded into the distance behind them, a low sprawl of wooden buildings and stockyards permeated by the odour of Xand hide. Gall ta Kereth maintained a steady pace, his huge animal—the same beast Spellbinder and Raven had watched in the combats—running tirelessly, willing to continue long after the three horses were winded and slowing down.

They rode from sun's rise to late evening, halting only to rest the horses or stretch saddle-wearied limbs. At night they camped beneath the open sky or found shelter with some local Xand herder in one of the fortified holdings that dotted the open grasslands like tiny villages. The terrain remained mostly flat, stretching away, green and feature-less, to the distant horizon so that the occasional stands of timber or the mesas that broke up the monotony of the landscape were welcome diversions.

Ta Kereth was perfectly at home, and Gondar—accus-tomed to lengthy ocean voyages—was at ease. Spell-binder and Argor, however, found the plains oppressive, curiously menacing in their uniformity. And in addition to this discomfort they felt a growing sense of depression as they rode farther westwards, as if the warm wind that blew from early morning until evening drained their resolution and seeded doubt in their minds. At first Gondar and Gall were not affected, but as they drew closer to the mountains the reiver and the Xand rider, too, began to show signs of discomfort.

Stronger and stronger grew this feeling, until they rode in miserable silence interrupted only by sudden outbursts of temper. Three times it was that Gondar and Gall came close to trading blows, and even Spellbinder was drawn into the bickering.

The warrior-wizard guessed that the evil known as Vedast was the source of the depression, for the cumulative effect was powerful enough to persuade any casual traveller to seek some brighter, more cheerful part of Xandrone. Yet he was unable to fight it: whatever force had denuded him of magical strengths in Haral was equally effective here; more so, for now it went farther than a mere stealing of strength.

One thing alone persuaded Spellbinder, Argor and Gondar to press on: the thought of Raven.

In the case of Gall ta Kereth it was a dogged determination to return home, the kind of blind resolution that prompts a homing bird to battle the storm, regardless of the cost.

And in time they saw the distant shapes of the World's End Mountains bulking against the sky.

Black were those hills, standing up like great jagged teeth from the green sward of the plains. Foothills ran out like great stone roots over the grass, as though the greater mass fed upon the land hulking above Xandrone's farthest boundaries as might some massive, somnolent beast that brooded on the commerce of the tiny, fragile creatures living about its rocky claw-roots. Trees and stunted shrubs covered the lower slopes, but higher up there was nothing, only the naked stone in all its many folds and crags. Bare and black, ominous, were the upper reaches. Snow blanched the highest peaks, and above them the sky was dark. No birds inhabited the trees, nor was there any sign of animal life.

Gall became increasingly disturbed as they drew closer to the holding of the Vanna clan.

The Hold was ringed by a high stockade, built back against a spur of rock that formed an impregnable wall to the rear. Gates of metal studded timber opened on to the grasslands, standing partially open so that the buildings inside the great wall were visible. They, too, were wooden, thick-walled with narrow windows and wide verandahs. A spring bubbled from the rock, filling a pool about which stood pens and barns. There was an oddly deserted air to the place.

"Ho!" shouted Gall as they approached the gates. "Gall ta Kereth comes home a champion! Is there no one to greet him?"

An old man shambled nervously towards the gate, supporting his weight on a pike that looked too heavy for him to wield. Along the catwalk of the wall there appeared more old men; women and children, too. They carried bows and throwing stars. They looked frightened. Spellbinder noticed that all were slow of movement or weak: they were either very old or very young, or crippled.

"Tambur?" Gall's voice was hushed to accommodate the silence, his boasting forgotten. "What has happened? Where is the clan?"

"Gone," said the old man. "Gone to cleaner pastures. And best you go, too."

Gall dismounted. "Best you explain first, Tambur."

They sat about a fire in one of the empty houses, drinking gryllar and tough, cured Xand meat. The night was warm enough within the walls that no heating was necessary; but the flames gave emotional warmth, stemming the shadows that flickered outside as the old man called Tambur spoke.

"It was after you had left for Haral, long enough that no messenger might hope to catch you and bring you back. At first it took only the weakest of the calves, but then it began to prey on the larger Xands. We sent men after it, thinking that some hunting beast had wandered over the mountains. The men did not come back." He paused, setting his fists together, palms uppermost and thumbs extended in the horn sign, the blessing against fear. "A greater party found the bodies: nine brave men, all ripped apart. We set traps then, and left men out to watch for what manner of beast it might be. They, too, died.

"One more party was sent, never to return. Then the creature came here. It slew three women and as many children, and when the men fought it their blades sank into it without harming the demon. Yet its claws were firm enough, for they rent two of the warriors before it departed."

"This demon," murmured Spellbinder, "what did it look like?"

"A great black thing," said Tambur. "Shaped akin to man, but different. It was taller even than your Kragg giant there. Black it was, with red eyes and glowing claws. It fought in silence, though its breath held the stink of an open midden and its very body seemed to ooze putrefaction. Stars sank into its hide as though dropped in mud, and when Zensa thrust a lance deep into its back the point went all the way through and hung there while the demon turned and plucked Zensa's stomach from his body."

"The thing that roamed Haral," nodded the magician. "Or one of its kin."

"And then?" urged Gall. "Did it drive the clan away?"

"It came three times more," sighed Tambur. "Though archers and starmen manned the walls, it still entered. After that, a Vedast priest came. A scrawny little thing, he was, riding a gelded Xand like a woman. He said he could rid us of the demon if we agreed to follow Vedast and set him higher than the Horn God. He said it was the time of Vedast. That the son overthrew Alavia and the Horn God and was our only saviour."

The old man chuckled, emboldened by the gryllar, and nodded sagely; appreciative.

"We slaughtered his Xand for meat. Then we turned him out to fend alone, but he would not go away. So we took him back in and sacrificed him to the Horn God in the old way. He made a great squealing as the horns went in, but it did no good. The demon came again and then again.

"Your father Taal decided that the clan should move away for a while. He took them north to Ghafa Hold. He decided the demon might go away if there was nothing to feed on here."

"You remain," said Gall. "You and the others. Why did he not take you?"

Tambur shrugged. "I am too old to go away and find a new place to live. The others here are the crippled or the weakling young. If we die, then we are no great loss to the clan. If we live, we shall be mighty among the Vanna Heroes."

He laughed. "It would be nice to be a hero, Gall. And

if not, then I think my ancient flesh must be too sinewy for
the demon's taste. I have seen it come again, and it has
seen me. But it never touched me.''

"It comes again, then?" asked Spellbinder. "How
often?"

"Of course it comes again," chuckled Tambur. "It
comes each night. But it no longer seeks flesh.''

Argor's hand reached for his sword. Gondar's found
war-axe. Gall's drew scimitar. Only Spellbinder remained
unmoving.

"It will come tonight," he said; flatly, not doubting.
"And it will know we are here.''

"Aye!" Gondar's voice was eager. "With axe and
sword enough to pluck even a demon's life.''

"No!" Spellbinder spoke sharply, his voice commanding. "Our blades cannot harm it. I fought this thing before, and I know it cannot be destroyed. We must go
away. Now! Go away and wait. Follow the thing.''

"This is not like you," said Argor. "I have known you
long and long, but never known you run from a battle.''

"The Lifebane does not know how to run," snarled
Gondar. "Except forwards, into battle.''

"I will not desert my Hold as my father has," said Gall.
"I would rather die here than give it up.''

"Raven!" Spellbinder's voice cracked like a whip over
the protestations. "Have you forgotten so easily why we
came here? We came to find her. This demon is a creature
of the thing that holds her. To find her we must find the
entrance to the lair. If the demon wanted Vanna Hold, it
would have taken it. It has not, so it must have some other
purpose. We go out and hide. Then follow the thing.''

"But what then?" asked Argor, reasonably. "Your magic
is gone in this place, so all we have left is the strength of
our swords. And where might Raven be in this place?"

"Aye, he speaks sense," said Gondar. "Without your
magic how can we find her? Let us at least take comfortable bed and honest battle. And if we die, then so it goes.''

"No! You are too ready to set sword and axe gainsaying
knowledge!" His tone was cool like a honed blade. "We
cannot kill this thing, this demon. Not with steel. We must
wait.''

"For what?" asked Gall ta Kereth, echoed by Gondar and Argor.

"For the messenger promised by the oracle of Ban," said Spellbinder. "Until then, we are helpless."

And there came, as though in answer to his words, a beating of wings beyond the windows, a rushing of sound and a great, dark shape that fluttered against the fire's light, night-black pinions gusting the fire's blaze backwards across the room.

"The bird!" Argor said. And Gondar: "Raven's messenger!" And Spellbinder: "The word!"

They rose and went outside to where the huge, dark shape perched upon the well's wall, and listened to its shrieking, strident in the night.

It lofted to the star-flecked sky and came down over the pen containing their riding animals, settling upon the saddle of Spellbinder's horse.

The dark man went over to the fence and thrust his arm out to make a perch for the bird, which stepped carefully along the limb until it was settled on his shoulder.

"Do you still doubt?" he asked. "Or will you insist on more convincing?"

Gondar's answer came by way of a rush to his horse, closely followed by Argor. Gall ta Kereth was slower, though still he came.

They set saddles upon their animals and rode out from Vanna Hold into the night, led by the bird which swooped and hovered before them until they were several klis from the walled holding.

They lit no fire that night, preferring to find what warmth they could in their blankets as they stared towards the holding and waited for sign of the demon.

None came, and when Gall ta Kereth rode out in the morning he brought back the news that the creature had merely examined the holding before departing into the hills.

The bird lofted, shattering the morning's quiet with its strident cries. It beat its wings about Spellbinder's head, starting towards the mountains then coming back to flutter the dark man's hair with the turmoil of its passage. Spellbinder stared up at the dark, avian shape, and said, "I think it is time to discuss the seer's riddle."

The bird, as though in answer, settled upon his shoulder again and began to preen itself. Spellbinder concentrated, anxious to recall the exact words of the oracle's chant.

"You must go where none can pass,
Where death's drear stone divides the grass.
Where sun and light and all life dies,
And corpses rot beneath the skies,
That once were blue."

"The Valley of the Dead!" Gall spoke quickly, interrupting the second stanza. "Our people are taken there when the Horn God claims them. It is a place shut in by high walls, so that no light shines upon them and nothing grows. It must be there!"

"Wait," said Spellbinder, "for there is more yet:

"Tread in fear where eyes are blind,
And death's dread demons stalk behind.
Beware the blade of foe and friend,
For life must cease before you end,
This journey."

"That part," said Gall, "I do not understand, but I will take you to the valley if you wish."

"We have no other place," said Gondar. "Unless we track this demon down."

"It must be there," said Argor. "That must be the place."

"We shall go there," said Spellbinder. "If it is the wrong place, then the bird will tell us."

They mounted again and rode towards the mountain. Towards the Valley of the Dead.

Thirteen

"Beware man, for the grave reaches out to bring you down."

The Books of Kharwhan.

The valley was a dark and sombre place.

It was reached by a narrow trail that wound up through the foothills along flanks of bare stone on which there grew no bees or shrubs, not even any grass. It was as though the world ended there, where the naked rock stretched up towards the sky, black stone on darker heavens. The farther they penetrated that gloomy passage, the darker was the firmament above them, until black met black and they moved through a kind of twilight lit only by the rays of an unseeable sun that streaked the stone with the colours of blood.

The mood of depression that had afflicted them as they approached Vanna Hold became stronger as they rode deeper into the mountains, thickening along with the shadows until it was almost irresistible, a palpable, horrible force through which they must press as through a curtain of spiders' webs. Fear and hatred danced in each man's mind so that they clutched their weapons, thinking alternately of the reassurance of a sturdy blade and the possibility of turning and using it on their friends as they fought clear of this awful place.

But they came at last to the valley, which was little wider than the trail entering it. And much, much worse.

It was a lengthy, narrow slit in the World's End Mountains; like a knife's cut in stony flesh. Sheer walls of black stone lifted up all around, leaping together at the highest points so as to cut out the dark, looming sky and leave the valley itself in perpetual night.

Grave markers dotted the arid grey soil of the floor, and

141

all about the rocky walls there were sealed caves containing more bodies.

The bird took perch on a crag overhanging the valley, shrieking a cry that sounded poised between warning and lament. The men rode in quietly, weapons drawn, and dismounted.

The place smelled of death. Of rotting bones and putrescent flesh. Here and there pieces of white stuck up from the spare soil: bones laid too shallow for the unfriendly earth to accept, and consequently thrust up again to rot in the pallid air of that awful place.

"Shroud of stone!" Argor clenched his fist in unfamiliar piety. "This place stinks of death. Is Raven here?"

"I think not." Spellbinder fought to keep his voice calm. "This is only the gateway to that place where she is held."

"Then let's go through. I can feel the bones pressing against me."

Even Gondar was awed by the dreadful valley.

And then, like some dark dream of night, the valley came to life.

From out of the ground there sprang skeletons in all their horrid grave clothes. Some were bare bones, others still reamed with tatters of flesh; yet more with robes and pieces of rotted armour. They reached up with gaping jaws and ragged fingers to pluck and snap at the riders. Worms fell from their vacant sockets. Earth cascaded from grinning mouths. Lumps of dripping flesh ran from ribs open to the reeking air.

Gall ta Kereth's scimitar cleaved skull from white neckbone. Gondar's great axe splintered skulls and breastbones alike in cleaving, downwards sweeps. Argor's straightsword hacked through rotten flesh and yellow ribs. And Spellbinder's blade of black Quwhonian steel cut clutching hands from bony wrists.

Yet the dead still pressed in. Fingers devoid of flesh reached out to pluck at living throats; gaping, maggotridden jaws snarled at swordhands; headless corpses with no right to live sought to smother warriors under their blanket of dead and reeking flesh.

And then the bird took flight again.

Like some portent of a greater doom it swept aloft, black wings beating fury down against the darker horror of the valley. It loosed one harsh and lonely scream and then was plummeting, wings folded, amongst the carnage.

Like a stooping hawk it dropped, fast and sure and savage. It fell betwixt the walls of rock and swooped with opening pinions over the fight. Spellbinder saw it as hands of bone closed about his throat. And saw the skull of the corpse-warrior torn away. Then saw it return to tear off an arm, and drop the bones across the valley, before returning again to rip away the second skeleton arm. It swirled and swooped as no mortal bird could ever fly, plucking off bones and skulls until all the grave-warriors were left in ruins, bloodless and bony and silent again.

Then it settled above an opening at the farther end of the valley, where a wide cave stared unseeing across the battlefield.

The men looked about them. And saw their animals gone down in bloody ruin. Gall ta Kereth wept at that, when he saw his Xand with the hide torn bloody from its ribs and the eyes gouged out, but the others wiped their blades and stepped forwards towards the hole the bird indicated; anxious for blood.

Then Gall ta Kereth let loose a great shout and ran headlong into the tunnel waving his scimitar like a madman, overtaking the others in his fury. He ignored Spellbinder's shouted warning and Gondar's clutching hands, and when Argor sought to trip him he clubbed the red-bearded mercenary with the hilt of his sword, leaving Argor bloody-nosed and stunned. At the entrance he paused, shaking his blade above his head and screaming a battle-cry.

And then he was gone into the darkness.

The others stared after him, simultaneously concerned for his safety and wary of charging blind into the ominous pit.

"What now?" asked Gondar. "Do we follow?"

"Aye," Spellbinder nodded. "We must."

He looked up to where the bird perched, his pale face creased in a frown. The bird's red eyes stared back, then it spread its wings and lifted from the rock, swooping down to settle again on Spellbinder's shoulder. It turned its

fierce head towards the cave's mouth and shrieked once.
The sound echoed about the Valley of the Dead, ringing
from the gloomy rock, reverberating back and forth until
the whole awful place was filled with the stridency.

And Spellbinder felt something reach out to touch his
mind and knew that he was not alone, nor powerless.

What help I can, I shall give. The soundless voice
rustled as might the wind through old bones. *Kharwhan
stands behind me, and I behind you. It may not be enough,
for under the mountain Vedast rules, but it is there. The
oracle of Ban is with you. Go forward.*

He set his silver shield more securely on his arm, hefted
the black sword, and stepped into the mouth of the pit.
Argor and Gondar followed behind.

It was dark. Not only was light absent from the hole,
but also there was a dark pressure, as though the sheer
weight of the rock above them pressed in, that and the
weight of the years, of ageless, timeless evil. Thick cobwebs brushed against their faces, and they felt the fleeting
touch of scuttling legs on those parts of their bodies not
protected by armour. Each man held his shield close against
his chest, the rim drawn up to cover neck and jaw, swordarm
thrust out to tap blade on rock like blindmen's canes. They
stumbled, feeling their way, ignoring the darting of arachnids, the nip of mandibles, the heavy cling of cobwebs
sticky with venom. And all the time a kind of echo rang in
their minds, saying "Go back! Go back! Or stay for
ever."

How long they fumbled in that horrible blackness they
could not tell, but then, abruptly, they came to a place
where dim red light illuminated a huge chamber.

The light appeared to emanate from a well at the centre
of the vault, as if the burning core of the world was tapped
to grant light to the place. There was the reek of sulphur
and decayed flesh, and a constant susurration of movement. The vault was roofed low, with dark, forbidding
passages leading off all round the sides. They could not
see the farther limits of the place, nor even make out
individual details, for the light shimmered and flickered,
deceiving the eye. The floor was flat and thick with grey
dust tinted crimson by the strange light, and though there

was no sign of Gall ta Kereth they could make out his footprints leading away across the chamber. Those and other, indefinable markings, as if sharp sticks had been dragged over the ashen surface.

Spellbinder halted, staring round; listening. On his shoulder, the black bird stirred restlessly.

"What is it?" Argor's voice was hushed. "What is that sound?"

It was quiet, scarcely loud enough to be discernible: a rustling as if grave vestments stirred faintly; a clicking; a barely audible stridulation.

"By the Mother!" Gondar set finger to thumb in the sign of the All-Mother's eye. "Let's follow on and be gone from here. I smell death here."

Spellbinder nodded, and stepped cautiously into the vault.

The dust was thick beneath their boots, warm like ashes, raising noxious clouds that clogged their throats and watered their eyes. As they progressed through the chamber the stink of sulphur grew stronger, the cloying air warmer.

Argor glanced warily at a side tunnel. And saw red orbs staring back. The clicking sound got louder. He shouted, "Beware!"

And a scuttling, darting thing, all legs and snapping mandibles, ran towards them.

It was a spider, but such a spider as they had never seen, not even in the Ishkarian Rift. It was mottled grey and red, blending with the rock, and it stood high as a man's waist. Where they were slowed by the clinging dust, the arachnid seemed to dance across the surface, balancing a bloated body on all its eight legs. Eyes like red jewels decorated the entire circumference of its head, some set forwards, others to the back or top or the underside. Huge mandibles snapped like shears about an orifice designed not to eat, but to suck out the essence of its victims, and at the rearward part of the body there curved a vicious sting.

It was on Argor before the echo of his warning died. He had barely time to swung his shield round before the mandibles snapped on his thigh.

They closed on the rim, and though the spider could not bite through the metal it still sprang up, the powerful, hairy legs launching the bloated body into the air so that Argor was hurled backwards, falling in the dust.

He stabbed the sword into the creature's head, slicing great cuts that dripped loathsome ichor, holding off the snapping, deadly mandibles with his shield as he kicked his legs in an attempt to avoid the tail sting; shouting all the while in horror at the vile attack.

Spellbinder and Gondar sprang to his aid. Sword of Quwhon steel severed grasping legs from grey blood; Kragg axe sank deep in thorax and belly sac. Stinking ichor spurted from the creature. Spellbinder cut the sting away, kicking it far across the vault; Gondar sliced axe deep into the featureless "face," leaving the mandibles still affixed to Argor's shield.

The loathsome body still twitched when they kicked it clear, though it was now legless and dripping. Argor climbed to his feet, face paled by the hideousness of the attack.

And more arachnids scuttled from their holes.

The three warriors set their backs together, forming a triangular defence. The bird beat its wings angrily about the red-lit vault, screaming its irritation.

The spiders attacked in two ways. Several would rush in to snap at legs and outthrust swords, seeking to rend flesh or tear away a blade; others jumped, using the bodies of their companions as launching platforms, off which they sprang through the air to hurl themselves at the heads of the three men.

Against the airborne attacks, the bird was the best defence. It flew in savage circles above Spellbinder and the others, using claws and beak to tear apart the arachnids. The others fell to sword and axe; it became apparent that a blow directed at the head, to strike where mandible joined jaw, was the best cut, sundering the muscles conjoining the pincers so that their strength was lost. Mostly, when cut that way, the spiders would withdraw, for it was in their obscene nature to first paralyse with the mandibles and then inject the venom of their stings. The few that attempted to pierce armour with the hooked point in the tail were quickly dealt with, the stinger being cut away after the mandibles, thus leaving the arachnid helpless.

Equally, the three men severed legs, finding that as good a defence as any; so long as they could cut off sufficient of the multiple limbs to render the spider motionless.

They were weary as the battle ended, and the floor of the cavern was thick with twitching bodies and the stink of ichor that blended with the sulphur to fill the atmosphere with a foul, fetid smell.

They moved quickly on as the last, wounded, spider scrabbled clear of the mounded bodies.

Gall ta Kereth found himself in an open place.

Behind, the mountains bulked up towards an open sky, blue streaked through with streamers of fluffy cloud like white banners in battle array. Ahead lay a meadow of lush grass, bounded by trees in such profusion as he had never seen. Down the slopes of the mountains ran rivulets that seemed to emerge from the snow-capped peaks and cascade over the rocks to feed the stream running through the meadow.

He paused, staring about him; wondering.

There was no sign of Spellbinder and the others, though he was sure they had been close on his heels when he ran into the cavern, and the passage from the Valley of the Dead to this luxuriant place had been short, unhindered by any of the attacks the warrior-mage had suggested might come. Yet now he stood in a garden, as pleasant as any he had seen in Xandrone.

He smiled, though still keeping his scimitar in his hand, and stepped out across the grass.

"I believe," said the Ketta, "that it is time to test you."

"What do you mean?" Raven was confused, suddenly more unsure of herself than ever before. "How will you test me? Surely you know what I feel."

"I have allowed entrance to limbo to one man." The blue-eyed creature smiled at her. "You must kill him to prove your loyalty."

"Who is he?" she asked. "Is he known to me?"

"His name," said the Ketta, "is Gall ta Kereth. Kill him and I shall know that I can trust you."

Raven nodded: if the spilling of one life's blood was needed to save the world, then it was a reasonable price. Besides, she felt there was no choice: if the Ketta had decided to pit her against this Gall ta Kereth, then the fight would come, whatever she might want. And if it resolved to single combat, then she would fight to live, no matter what.

"Give me your hand," he said.

She took it, and again the light flickered into non-light. And they stood in a clearing, fronting a stream beyond which there lifted the steep flanks of blackstone mountains, banded at the upper levels by snow and cloud.

Across the grass there was a man. He was a head shorter than she, but banded heavily with muscle. His legs were bowed, wrapped round with tough Xand leather; his torso was protected by a cuirass of the same hide, a bandoleer of throwing stars forming an X shape that glinted in the light. His head was bare, exposing long, greasy hair that straggled over broad shoulders, the arms girded with plates of metal and Xand leather. He carried a round buckler on his left arm and a vicious scimitar in his right hand.

"Kill him," said the Ketta. "Kill him and prove yourself."

Gall ta Kereth saw the woman emerge from the forest and knew she was a demon. Perhaps the one that had preyed on his people, disguised now, but still the same malevolent spirit that owed him so many lives.

He shouted his battle-cry—"Vanna! Vanna and ta Kereth!"—and charged forwards.

Raven took the charge on her sword's point, blocking the downswing of the scimitar with the sleeve-shield as she cut across with the Tirwand blade.

Sparks flew where scimitar struck metal, and sliced leather burst from Gall's buckler.

They parted, each one appraising the other's skill; probing for weakness, assessing strengths. Raven's blade was longer, and her greater height afforded her the longer reach, but she was protected only by the Ishkarian shield and scanty chainmail. Gall was shorter, but armed with a curved blade that might easily catch an arm, and his buckler hid his torso and belly, which in turn were swathed in leather and metal.

He cut in, seeking to hook Raven's legs from under her, at the same time blocking her stroke with the leathern shield.

Raven darted back, setting distance between them with her blade.

Gall took the sword on his buckler slicing the scimitar over the roundel to stilke at her head. Raven crouched beneath the blow, deflecting it with the sleeve-shield. Then felt the shield tugged forwards as the recurved hook of the scimitar caught in the underside, dragging her off balance.

At the same time, Gall's buckler smashed down against her head, the metal bosses crunching into her skull with numbing force. Her eyes sparkled bright flashes of light and only battle-trained reflex turned her body to roll beneath the blow, instinct telling her that the scimitar was still caught in her shield and so might be dragged downwards.

She fell and turned, pulling the Xandronian champion with her. At the same time she drove her own blade upwards, cutting under Gall's buckler to pierce the leather girding his loins.

She felt the tip go in and continued rolling, lifting her legs to plant both feet in the man's stomach and tip his body over, raising it above her own in a culmination of downwards, unbalanced momentum and upwards kick.

Gall ta Kereth shouted in surprise and sudden fear. He felt himself lifted up, then the warm slicing of the blade through his flesh. He sought to free his scimitar, but was unable, for Raven was hauling down on the hook, pinning the blade.

She sensed Gall above her at the apex of her kick. And dropped her feet. The result was to leave the Xandronian in the air, balanced on the point of her sword. His own weight did the rest: he settled on to the blade like a fly pinned against a wall. Blood spurted from his belly, splattering over Raven's face as he slid down the length of the gem-hilted sword.

Raven twisted her arm, spilling the body sideways, turning her shield free of the scimitar to slam the point in against the man's neck.

The sword's tip emerged bloody from Gall ta Kereth's back, and at the same time the point of the Ishkarian sleeve-shield severed his jugular vein. He voiced one last cry before his life bubbled frothy from his mouth: "Vanna! And ta Kereth!"

Raven turned, kicking the body clear of her sword. She rose to her feet, wiping blade and shield on the grass, glaring towards the forest, from where came the Ketta.

"Well done," he smiled. "You are truly a champion worthy of my favour."

"Have I proved myself?" she asked, wiping blood from her face. "Am I now deemed loyal?"

"Loyal enough, though one test remains."

"Which is?" She sheathed her sword, staring at him. "What is the final test?"

"Take my hand," he said softly. "I shall explain it to you later."

Beyond the vault of the spiders there was a long, wide tunnel lit with blue luminescence. Niches were carved at intervals along the walls and in each alcove there was a mummified body. They were unhuman, those corpses, with wide staring sockets set at angles to the thin, empty bones of the nostrils. The jaws were narrow, vee-shaped, with triangular teeth that were sharp at the edges and pointed at the tips.

And as Spellbinder led the way down the tunnel the bare skulls turned to follow the trio's passage.

At the end light glinted faintly, then was blocked by a massive shape that hulked there, waiting.

It was though a vacuum existed, for there was no clear defining of it, only a hint of body with glowing eyes and phosphorescent talons, gleaming fangs.

Spellbinder recognised the demon of Haral.

"We must go round it," he said. "I know not how, but we must."

Gondar roared, swinging his axe about his head in flailing circles. Spellbinder shouted ''No!'' but the giant sea-reiver was already charging headlong at the creature.

Argor paused long enough to shout, ''Go round! We'll hold it.'' Then himself was racing after Gondar.

Spellbinder felt the bird leave his shoulder and mouthed a curse even as his legs pounded the dry rock and he threw himself into the hopeless battle.

Gondar's axe clove through dark, stinking flesh. Dribbling putrescence flowed from the thing's neck. It roared, striking out at the blonde-maned reiver, its talons striking his shield to hurl him back. Argor ran in, cutting low to hamstring the monster. And found his blade slicing incorporeal rottenness. His blow met so little resistance that he spun round, unbalanced as the creature's claws tore links of mail from his back.

Spellbinder saw the bird fluttering above a stream that ran across the ground before the tunnel's exit, screaming and beating its wings over the water. As though calling him, it flew back to flap about his head, then returned to the stream, swooping low enough that its claws broke the surface. Then it returned to the mouth of the tunnel, flapping about the head of the demon as Gondar and Argor swung useless blades against the nebulous might of the black body.

Droplets touched the thing, and it screamed, forgetting the fight as water burned like fire about its indistinct face.

Realisation dawned on Spellbinder, and he shouted, ''Leave it! Do not fight it! Run!''

Argor was the first to understand him, picking himself up from the rocky floor with crimson staining his armour and a great purple bruise down half his face. Gondar was slower, and so took a vicious cut along his left arm before he broke clear and splashed into the stream.

The bird fluttered about the demon's head, beating wings and darting beak against the black substance of the thing's face, slashing talons like sickles at red eyes and gaping, roaring mouth.

Spellbinder sprang back over the water, capering before the monster as he shouted taunts and swung his sword.

A slashing paw caught his shield, hurling him backwards with sheer brute force. He flew through the air, landing on his back in the stream. And the demon, unthinking, charged after him.

Its massive paws reached out, all hooked talons, gleaming and bright. Its mouth gaped to expose great fangs that ran with dripping saliva. Its eyes were bright and red and furious.

And then they closed. And a hideous wailing burst from the open maw. And the monster fell down on its knees, slashing at the water as though it sought to wipe away the stream.

And with each splashing of its paws it poured more water over its body, and screamed more hideously, for the water seemed as acid on its hide, dissolving whatever substance it was formed from so that it began to dissolve before their eyes, rotting away as might mud in heavy rain.

"Quick!" Spellbinder called. "Drench it! Kill it!"

They staggered to the edge of the stream and cupped their hands to rain water over the beast that wailed and writhed in the centre of the rivulet. And each fresh splashing seemed to burn away more of its body, until it fell down, seething, into the water, and was torn apart and floated away.

And then they rested for a while, checking their surroundings, for it seemed that they had passed the worst of Vedast's guardians and were come to his central place.

Which was horrible as the outer trails.

Behind them there lifted up a great black wall of rock, smooth and sheer, like dark glass, its only break the mouth of the tunnel through which they had recently come. The stream curved round the opening, running away into the distance over a flat plain of ashen grey. There were no trees, no grass. There was nothing but that vast expanse of grey, dead earth.

The sky was leaden; colourless. No sun shone, nor any clouds broke the unending expanse of flat, dead heavens that seemed to reach down to join the flat, dead land.

The soil was dry and cold, like old ashes. There was no visible distinction between land and sky, and the dark bulk of the gloomy hills appeared to curve round on all sides so that distance was unjudgeable, everything melding into a single great bowl of greyness that might have been an arm's length distance, or days of walking.

One feature alone distinguished that awful, unborn nullity.

Far away—or so it seemed—there was a solitary tower. White like old bone reached up from drear earth to lifeless sky, about the highest level, a corpse-yellow dome.

Spellbinder pointed towards the lonely obelisk.

"She must be there," he said. "Come, let's find her."

Fourteen

"What is death? Death is what you make it, man. For it is only the manner of your dying that is important."
Xand Riders' Song.

The Ketta studied the jewels covering the surface of the black shelf, then turned towards the windows. This time there was no rolling of the mist, no vision of the future, instead there was a magnification of the outer world, a telescoping of vision that granted access to the farthest reaches of his domain. He led Raven away from the door, striding round the circular chamber to indicate a section of window directly across from the door.

It was though she perched on the highest limbs of a tall tree, looking down at the ground. She saw the stream and the meadow where she had fought Gall ta Kereth, but there was now no sign of the body, only three familiar figures trudging purposefully across the grass.

"Spellbinder!" She gasped in surprise. "Argor and Gondar with him."

"No doubt come to save you," the Ketta murmured. "You must be flattered at such attention."

He glanced at her, and she held her face impassive only with difficulty, fearful of revealing the excitement she felt. Seeking to obscure her confusion she asked a question.

"How came they here? I thought your guardians too strong to pass? I thought only the one man was granted entrance?"

The Ketta frowned; for a moment there came black hinting of his non-human image, but then it was gone again, replaced by the blandly smiling features that were, all at the same time, handsome, sardonic and menacing.

"Your companion is blessed with power." His voice was thoughtful, almost doubting. "Something aids him, though it cannot be Kharwhan for I have established too

154

many barriers against the Ghost Isle's strength. It must be something else.''

He broke off, staring at the trio now moving into the shelter of the forest. There was a lack of decision about his movements, subtly apparent in his face, that gave Raven cause to wonder at his ability to halt the intrusion. So far as she could tell, he was genuinely surprised to see the three men; nor certain what to do about them. She waited.

''I might kill them now,'' he said. ''Easily. But I think not. I told you of the final test: they shall be that resolution. I had something else in mind, but that can come later. As pleasure.''

''What would you have me do?'' Raven asked.

''Why,'' smiled the Ketta, ''it shall be a simple thing. Kill Spellbinder.''

Beyond the edge of the stream there were the marks of battle. The dead, grey ash was stirred with footsteps, hollowed by rolling bodies. One set of prints—presumably belonging to Gall—emerged from the water, then became deeper, as though he had run forward to meet whoever made the second set that began a little distance off and ended where the two trails met. The ash was scuffed about, and there was the marking of falling bodies, a dark patching, as if blood had spilled. There was no sign of Gall, nor any other trail.

''What took him?'' Gondar wiped at the blood still oozing from his lacerated arm. ''How can it leave no sign?''

Spellbinder shrugged. ''No natural law applies here, my friend. We walk in limbo between life and something else.''

''And we have, it seems, a long walk with little water,'' said Argor practically. ''I have a water bag that may last the three of us a day, perhaps a little longer. How far away is that dismal place?''

Spellbinder looked towards the gloomy tower. ''I am not sure,'' he said, ''but there is a way to find out.''

''Aye,'' nodded Argor. ''We walk it.''

They started off over the blank, featureless plain, each step pluming dust about their feet so that they moved in a

kind of mist, leaving behind a grey wake that settled
slowly back into their footprints, gradually hiding all signs
of their passing.

It was as though they traversed a dream, when each step
taken seems to leave the dreamer two back, and limbs
move with unreal slowness, emphasising the futility of effort. Although they trudged onwards for long enough that
even Gondar's mighty legs grew weary, they seemed,
when they halted, no closer to the tower than when they
had started. They stopped before their strength gave out,
seeking to husband reserves of energy in anticipation of
struggle, and settled to a cold and miserable camp.

There was no opportunity to build a fire, for the plain
remained blank and flat and featureless, showing nothing
but the grey, cold ash. The sky above them—if sky it
was—shared that same implacability: looming grey and
bleak and forbidding. There was no night, nor any real
day, only the continuation of dismal grey light, unchang-
ing. It was hard to see through the gloom and equally hard
to sleep. They arranged a rota of watches, and Argor took
the first while the others wrapped arms about their heads
and settled into the dust.

The bird scrabbled irritably in the lifeless soil for a
while, then took flight, winging fast in the direction of the
tower.

Raven ate that night—if night it was—with the Ketta, in
the great banqueting hall. She was anxious to know what
his next move might be, but wary of arousing his suspicions by asking him directly: she chose to rely on flattery
to discover his purpose.

"There is no point to destroying them yet," he said in
answer to one question. "Of course I could, but my
designs encompass a greater fold of this reality than you
can imagine. Spellbinder must die; and you must kill him.
But the others are useful. Taken alive, their minds may be
shaped to my purpose; used, as I shall use that Xandronian
you slew for me."

"And when shall we ride out?" she asked meekly.
"When shall we conquer in your name?"

"Soon," he said. "I'd first have Spellbinder here. Even

dead, his mind may yield up secrets. That first, then the conquering.''

Later that ''night,'' when a more natural-seeming darkness than had previously shrouded her chambers was fallen, she lay sleepless on the great bed, pondering. She was naked, though her sword was beside the couch and her armour stood ready nearby. And there intruded on her thoughts a familiar sound: as of wings beating, the tap of beak against windowpane.

She rose and crossed to the window, throwing it wide open.

The bird was perched on the sill. It entered the room, fluttering to the bed. Raven reached out to stroke the glossy head comforted by its presence, waiting for it to impart some message.

When the words came, they were indistinct, as though filtered through background noise, faint, as might be a voice speaking softly in a fog, close to the sea's shore when the waves pound against the land.

Ready . . . stand ready . . . Soon . . . Death . . . there must be . . .

''I cannot understand,'' she whispered. ''What must be?''

Fight . . . Spellbinder . . . Argor . . . Gondar . . . Death . . . Death rules . . . You must find the way . . . High . . . Trick death . . . Live . . . Lives . . . Think . . . You must . . .

Then it was gone in a black beating of wings that stirred the covers of the bed and left her mind in doubt, confused. She stared out of the window, unable to spot the creature against the darkness of the forest, wondering what it had meant, what message it had sought to impart.

She stretched on the wrinkled covers, eyes closed tight and mind troubled. Finally she slept.

There was no morning in that grey place, no change in the texture of the light or the cloying, oppressive atmosphere. They deemed it ''morning'' simply because the sleepers woke and all were rested as best they could hope. They swallowed a little water from Argor's bag and set out again, trudging in silence towards the tower.

How many klis they had covered, they could not say: the greyness hid the mountains behind them and the tower seemed no closer. The place was truly limbo, for motion became pointless, it seemed, not bringing them anywhere, merely tiring them and depressing them. Yet still they marched resolutely onwards.

They slept again when they were weary enough, sharing out the last of the water, and rose again, and walked. Silent, almost unthinking.

The bird returned, settling on Spellbinder's shoulder, its talons gripping hard against his armour.

And it was as though the avian's presence granted him perspective, for he was suddenly able to see the tower clearly. He saw that it was little more than a kli distant, resting on a great mound of dark stone about which there was a deep, blackened pit. The walls of the column were scarred and blackened, as if fierce flame had played over the surface, and from amongst that pitted tracery there thrust out protuberances that might have been either windows or guardposts or balconies; it was impossible to tell. At the base of the tower was a door wide enough that five men might enter standing shoulder to shoulder, and it was equally high. A kind of drawbridge, or ramp, extended from the base of the door, spanning the pit.

Spellbinder led the way towards that bridge.

"The time approaches," said the Ketta. "They will be here soon. Are you ready?"

Raven nodded: "I am ready."

"Good," said the Ketta. "Wait here, in the hall. When the time comes, I shall bring him to you."

He stood up, pushing back his chair, and left her alone in the great empty banqueting room with the light streaming in through the multi-coloured windows as if to illumine her doubts and make brighter still her fears.

Spellbinder reached the bridge and halted. Gondar stood to his right, Argor to his left. They both, now, could see the tower clearly, and wondered at its melancholy aspect, the curious nature of the thing.

RAVEN 5: A TIME OF DYING   159

"No fortress I have seen," said Argor, "ever looked like this."

"It appears metallic," added Gondar. "Yet who—or what—can build in metal?"

"Vedast rules in limbo," said Spellbinder. "And in limbo all things are possible."

He turned his eyes to the bird, still perched upon his shoulder, and then stepped forwards onto the bridge. His boots rang loud on the studded surface, a weird contrast to their silent progress through the grey ash.

The door opened.

Gondar set his hand more firmly about the leather-wrapped haft of his great axe, tugging the retaining loop firmer about his wrist and balancing the curved head on the flat of his left palm.

Argor brought his shield round to protect his chest, canting his sword over his right shoulder.

Spellbinder shrugged, dislodging the bird which beat upwards to circle their heads as the warrior-wizard unsheathed the blade of black, Quwhon steel, his breath whistling harsh through the confines of his silver helm.

And Gall ta Kereth stepped out to meet them.

His dark eyes were blank, one yet clogged with dry blood from a cut above his brow. A bruise darkened the swarthiness of his face on the left side, and about his lower belly and down his inner thighs, his armour was stained with old, dried crimson. Across his neck there opened the lips of a great, savage rent; dull brown was that secondary mouth, with dribbles of the same colour staining neck and shoulder. He carried his head to one side, as though seeking to hold the wound closed. On his left arm he carried a round buckler of sword-cut leather; in his right hand, the recurved scimitar.

"None may pass," he said. And his voice was dry as the clotted blood upon his body. "It is not allowed."

With that, he charged forwards, swinging his scimitar in clumsy sweeps that were easy to avoid.

Spellbinder ducked beneath his blows, but Gondar slid his axe clear of his hand and began to twirl the blade, preparatory to decapitation.

Spellbinder shouted, "No! Gondar! Leave him be!"

The axe cut air close enough to Gall's head that the hair fluttered upwards in its passing. And the Xandronian stumbled by, scimitar still swinging as he faltered past them and stumbled to a stop, turning, then coming back across the bridge.

"Golem!" shouted Spellbinder. "Vedast has taken his mind! Leave him live. Stun him."

Argor stepped out to block the clumsy swings of the Xandrone scimitar with his shield, and Spellbinder swung the flat of his blade down hard against Gall's skull. The Vanna-man crumpled to his knees, dropping his blade. Gondar ended the work with the nub of his axe, slamming it down onto Gall's head so that the clansman—the golem—slumped flat on the dusty surface of the bridge.

"There's little enjoyment in such bloodless combat," said Gondar. "Does all this effort result only in breaching a tomb?"

His question was boastful, covering his worry. Spellbinder recognised it as such, and said:

"No. Our effort is still to free Raven. And that will take all our effort! What comes next must be the hardest."

They entered the tower.

There was a narrow corridor beyond the entry hall, bright with illumination that seemed to shine from walls and floor and roof alike. The tread of their footsteps was loud, like naked metal; metal on metal: the clash of steel blade against steel shield. The bird flew out before them, halting at a door.

They shoved it open and saw Raven seated at a great table, her blade spread over the wood between plates of food.

And phantasmagoric tendrils of dark vapour seized hold of Argor and Gandor, wrapping about their arms and legs and torsos to hold them still, weapons useless in their hands as Raven climbed to her feet and lifted her sword, saying, "He is here."

And the Ketta emerged smiling from the shadows. And said, "Kill him, then."

Abruptly, like the glint of sun on sword as it flashes before the enemy's eye, there appeared a pillar of dark marble standing up from the wooden floor. Manacles sprouted like branches from the column, encircling Spellbinder's wrists and ankles so that he was held helpless, motionless, arms dragged back to expose chest and belly and legs to the cut of her blade.

"Kill him," repeated the Ketta. "Put your sword in his gut and spill his life out. End the dominance of Kharwhan now. Now!"

Raven lifted her sword, balancing its weight.

Spellbinder stared at her, his eyes blue; expressionless.

"Do it," he said. "Now!"

Raven sprang forwards, grasping the hilt in both hands so as to add extra weight to the blow.

The shining blade of Tirwan steel came down in a hissing arc, like the fangs of a striking snake: straight at Spellbinder's face.

Gondar shouted an inarticulate cry of rage and hate and despair.

Argor roared, "No! No, Raven!"

Her blade turned at the last moment, slicing away from the dark man's face to sunder the chains pinning his right arm against the pillar. Then cut back above his head to cleave through the second manacle, splitting it as might a knife cut butter.

The Ketta screamed in rage, but Raven ignored his shouting, directing her blows to the cutting of Spellbinder's ankle chains.

The Ketta changed shape, losing all semblance of humanity as black roaring unflesh replaced the golden body in horrid, snarling fury.

"Bitch! Betraying, loathsome bitch!" The voice belled through the hall. "You shall die! All of you! All die!"

Raven felt herself thrust aside by an arm that struck her ribs and lifted her as easily as a straw, tossed her away as the Ketta snarled and gibbered, reaching out to sink claws into Spellbinder's body.

"Death! I am death! I will visit you all!" The Ketta became black fire, reaching out to clutch Spellbinder as the dark warrior found his sword. "Die, humans! All of you! Die!"

The bird appeared then, sweeping down from the shadowy reaches of the hall to flash talons and beak in the

Ketta's face. It gave Spellbinder time enough to grasp his blade and turn to where his fellow warriors were still held against the wall.

The Ketta stumbled back under that attack, and Spellbinder wove his hands through the air in a mystic pattern, mouthing at the same time words too low and growling to be discernible.

The strange tendrils holding Argor and Gondar dissolved and they both ran forwards to join the fight.

The Ketta reached up, catching the black bird by one leg, dragging the avian down towards slavering jaws that sprouted gleaming fangs dripping with yellowish venom. Joining Spellbinder and the bird, Argor and Gondar set to hacking at the creature, so that it released the entrapped leg and the bird was able to fly towards the ceiling of the room, which now flickered into nebulous grey light.

Its hands released from the bird's leg, the Ketta turned to fighting the men, roaring and striking at their dancing blades.

Argor was thrown back, his shield split apart by a single blow of the Ketta's hand. Gondar cut in with his axe, only to find it blocked by a backswinging paw. Spellbinder thrust his blade into the creature's body, then darted free to shout at Raven.

"You know the secret of its power! Do what the bird told you! Swift, now, else we all die!"

Even as he said it, the Ketta turned up, grasping him about the waist to lift him up above that ravening head. He cut down at the arms and shoulders, writhing madly, but still unable to tear free even though Argor and Gondar swung sword and axe against the thing's body, raining blows in such profusion as would have hewn down any mortal thing.

"I do not know!" Raven's voice was lifted in a scream of fear and frustration and anger; all mingled. "Where?"

"Follow the bird!"

Spellbinder's voice choked off as the Ketta tossed him across the room as might a child throw away some unwanted toy.

Raven looked to where the bird was fluttering about the doorway, and ran towards it.

The Ketta moved to block her, bellowing its rage, but

Argor and Gondar interposed their bodies and their blades across its path, affording her passage, even at the cost of vicious wounds.

Unthinking, following the bird, she ran into the corridor; followed it to the low arch fronting the spiral stairway.

There the bird halted, screaming at her until she set foot on the first step, then winging back towards the hall and the sound of fighting.

She raced up the stairs, her mind dizzying as she made the turns lifting to the tiny platform fronting the black door.

It was open: she went inside the circular chamber.

The windows were blank again, milky white, showing only opalescent nothingness. She stared around, wondering what she was meant to do; then remembered the attention the Ketta had placed on the jewels surmounting the strange black shelf.

Systematically, using the hilt of her sword, she pounded the bright colours to dull, splintered fragments. She worked her way around the circular chamber, smashing each jewel until there was not one left shining; until all the flat, black shelf was littered with pieces and the dome shook as if trembled by an earthquake.

She ran back down the stairs.

And the Ketta met her at the foot.

All semblance of humanity was gone from him now, leaving only a great, dark shape akin to that ravening demon she had fought in Haral's combat field.

"Traitor!" it shouted. "Betrayer!"

She swung her sword to cut its belly, but the Ketta jumped aside, striking her blade away. Its paws—clawed now—reached for her. And would have found her, would have torn her had the bird not settled upon its skull and dug talons deep and harsh into the eyes so that it lurched back, dabbling at oozing, ichorous sockets.

"Raven! Fast now!" She heard Spellbinder's shout. "With us, quick!"

She cut once more at the Ketta, then ran down the corridor as the alien creature bellowed and staggered blindly up the staircase.

Spellbinder grasped her hand—a welcome touch of real

flesh—and dragged her towards the door she had not previously seen. Gondar and Argor and the bird followed behind, pausing only long enough to take the body of Gall ta Kereth with them.

They crossed the bridge, which began to rise even as they sprang clear and ran over the clinging ash. Briefly she was confused by the ground, for she had expected to find trees, grass, not this dead, dry greyness. But then Spellbinder pushed her down, shouting, "Cover your eyes!"

As he said it the tower shifted.

Ir was as though the entire column lifted up from its foundations, emitting a gust of withering flame that scorched about the pit she had seen as a moat. That was the last she saw, for afterwards everything was blotted out in a searing flash of brilliant light, as though a sun exploded and drenched the world in unseeable luminescence.

There was heat and a scorching absence of air, and when she opened her eyes again, there was only darkness; that and a great rending, creaking sound, as if the world moved and fell in upon itself.

Then a gust of fetid air blocked her nostrils and her eyes and her ears, and the ground seemed to smash upwards against her body, tossing her as casually as a child might lob a shuttlecock from hand to hand. And the roaring sound went on and on, gusting against her so that she was deafened and numbed and blinded.

The first thing she saw when finally she worked the dust from her eyes was the bird. It sat preening itself, running hooked beak down the feathers of its wings, wiping filth from the pinions and dropping the muck into the dark ground.

She stood up, Spellbinder and Argor and Gondar beside her, and looked back at Vedast's tower.

It was gone down into ruin, like an aged tombstone cracked and broken by the wind. What she had seen as vine-clad walls were now dark, pitted chunks of broken metal. The glowing golden dome was a shattered, splintered shell of dull glass. A great scorch mark blackened one side, extending out over the withered ground surrounding the place. Smoke rose from innumerable cracks in the structure, and even as she watched, sections of the thing collapsed inwards with rending signs of tortured fabric.

"What was it?" she asked, leaning on Spellbinder's arm. "What was the Ketta?"

"Death," he said. "Death, in one of his disguises."

"And is he gone now?"

"I think so." The warrior-magician pointed out over the terrain that was now become bleak and craggy, as though they stood not in a forest, nor yet in that grey desert, but at the centre of a valley in the World's End Mountains. "It is gone for the moment."

"But he—it—may come again?" asked Raven.

"Death always comes again," murmured Spellbinder. "So it goes."

Epilogue

"You leave a deal unsaid, old man."

The youngest of the merchants was caught up with the tale despite himself; the rambling narrative had trapped him as might a spider's web catch the attention of a fly, first attracting the insect, then holding it in the sticky strands; helpless.

"There is much that must go untold." The old man smiled slowly, the movement of his lips emphasising the wrinkles lining his withered face. *"Is any story ever truly finished?"*

"You speak in riddles." The eldest of the merchants upended his cup, tossing the dregs of the wine over the grass. He reached for a new skin, testing the sour vintage before passing the sack to his companions. "Every tale must have an ending, just as it must have a beginning. And a middle. Otherwise there is no story."

"Of course," smiled the oldster. *"But must it always be in that order?"*

"Riddles on riddles." The third man spoke. "Like a fall of rain clouding ditchwater: the one stirs the other, obscuring all."

"If all were clear," said the old man, *"life would become tedious. If it were possible to say where each footstep must fall there would be no joy in travelling. If you could foresee every action, foretell each event, would you not grow bored? Must everything be defined clearly?"*

"There is some sense in what you say," admitted the oldest of the listeners, "though were we able to foresee in that way, then we should be rich men. Not skulking in this stinking jungle."

"But the story remains unfinished," insisted the younger man. This champion of Xandrone—Gall ta Kereth? What became of him? He was killed, yet lived. What happened to him?"

"*Gall lived on.*" The old man stroked the bandages covering his severed hand. "*If you want a neat ending, then Gall ta Kereth was taken home over the peaks of the World's End Mountain, back to Vanna Hold. There he was healed of his wounds and restored to true life. The power of Kharwhan did that much for him, and all the rest he did himself.*"

"And Raven? Spellbinder? Argor and Gondar? What of them?"

The young merchant fiddled with the hilt of his rusted sword, seeking to hide his interest.

"*They carried Gall's body over the mountains. It was a dreadful journey that deserves a separate telling, for those peaks were high and bleak and lonely; the domain of beasts and men little better than beasts. But they took him back and went their separate ways. Gondar Lifebane took ship for Kragg and reived the seas a time longer; Argor travelled eastwards and south, to the Wastes. The others went about their own business.*"

"And Vedast? Was he truly dead? What was he?"

"*He died,*" murmured the old man, "*that was certain. But he might also have risen again, for it is hard to kill death. As to what he was . . . Well, he was many things. Most of all he was different—and men do not enjoy difference.*"

"But that is no reason to kill." Doubt sounded in the young merchant's voice; confusion. "Because a thing is different does not mean it must be destroyed."

"*You begin to learn. There is hope for you yet.*"

"I hope only for sleep," grunted the leader of the merchants. "I hope these damnable flies will cease their biting, and I hope we can clear this stinking jungle on the morrow. I hope we meet some village ready to buy our goods. Beyond that, my hopes end."

The old man nodded without speaking, stretching out on the ground beside the rivulet, eyes closed tight and arms wrapped about the gem-hilted sword. As though to set an ending on his story, night crept over the forest.

But for a long time the young man stared into the darkness, remembering.